Raiders of the Panhandle

By the same author

Billy Dare
Bodie
The Long Trail
The Trouble Hunter
Danger Valley
Showdown at Deadman's Gulch
Branagan's Law
Law of the Noose
Marshal of Borado
Valley of Fear
Buzzards in the Sky
The Man From Dodge
Brady's Revenge
Trail Dust
The Range Robber
Trail of the Killer

Raiders of the Panhandle

ALAN IRWIN

A Black Horse Western

ROBERT HALE · LONDON

© Alan Irwin 2000
First published in Great Britain 2000

ISBN 0 7090 6714 3

Robert Hale Limited
Clerkenwell House
Clerkenwell Green
London EC1R 0HT

Typeset by
Derek Doyle & Associates, Liverpool.
Printed and bound in Great Britain by
WBC Book Manufacturers Limited, Bridgend.

To Yvonne

ONE

As Jim Cochrane approached the buildings of the
Diamond R Ranch, a medium-sized spread in the
Texas Panhandle, north of Amarillo, he eyed them
with interest.

They consisted of a two-storey house, a cookshack, bunkhouse, barn and sheds, all with a
solid, well-finished look about them. A neatly
fenced corral stood well away from the buildings.

The ranch belonged to Will Ranger, a friend of
Jim's father, Tom Cochrane, who owned a big
spread south of Pueblo in Colorado. Will and Tom,
serving together in the Union Army during the
Civil War, had become close friends. When peace
finally came they both married and made their
separate ways west.

Jim's father had told him of the occasion,
during the war, when he had been knocked unconscious by enemy fire, and Will Ranger, under
heavy fire himself, had managed to carry him
back to the safety of their own lines.

7

The two men had kept in touch and Tom had been saddened to hear that just a few months earlier, in a riding accident, Will had so severely damaged his spine that he was now confined to a wheelchair for most of his waking hours.

After helping his father on the Colorado ranch for a spell, Jim, for the past three years, had been serving as a county sheriff in East Colorado, but feeling like a change of scenery he had decided to ride into Texas and try for a job with the Texas Rangers, a force he had long admired from afar.

As Jim's route took him close to the Diamond R, his father had asked him to look in on his old friend and see how he was faring.

As Jim headed for the ranch house, in the late afternoon, a hand who had just walked out of the barn stopped and stared at him, then ran over to the house, knocked on the door, and went inside.

When Jim reached the house minutes later, the door opened and the hand came out, followed by a big man in his fifties, bearded and just under six feet tall. The man was seated in a wheelchair, with a Winchester rifle laid across his knees. He stopped just outside the door. From his father's description, Jim knew that he was looking at Will Ranger.

Ranger looked hard at Jim. He saw a man in his twenties, a little above average height, well built, wearing a Colt .45 Peacemaker in a right-hand holster and a 10-inch Bowie knife on his belt. The stranger looked like he could take care of himself, but there was nothing menacing about him as he looked amiably at the rancher.

Looking back at Ranger, Jim got the impression that he was a very worried man. His brow was furrowed and there was a look almost of despair in his eyes.

'Who are you?' he asked Jim abruptly.

'Jim Cochrane,' said Jim. 'My father, Tom Cochrane, asked me to drop in on you as I was riding by, to see how things were with you, and to pass on his regards. He often talks of the time you two spent together in the Union Army.'

'So,' said Ranger, 'you're Tom's boy. I might have knowed it. You sure do favour him. Come on in.'

Jim dismounted and the hand took the reins of his horse and led it away. Jim followed the rancher into the house and through into the living-room, where his wife Emily was sitting. He introduced her to Jim. She was a handsome woman, slim and vivacious-looking, but on her face was the same strained look which Jim had discerned on the face of her husband.

'Tom told me in one of his letters,' said Ranger, 'that you were a lawman in Colorado.'

'That's right,' said Jim, 'but I felt like a change. I'm on my way to Amarillo, to join up with the Texas Rangers.'

Ranger looked at his wife. She stared back at him. He beckoned her and they left the room together. Sensing that something was very wrong,

Jim awaited their return. They came back into the room ten minutes later.

'I'm sorry about that,' said Ranger. 'You must think we're both plumb loco. The thing is, we're in deep trouble and weren't sure whether we could tell you about it. But now we both think we should. Maybe you can help us.'

The rancher went on to tell Jim of the entirely unforeseen catastrophe which had befallen the family on the previous day. He said he had been out on the range on a buckboard to look at a number of sick cows suffering from some sort of skin disease. Two of his hands had accompanied him, another hand was working on a different section of the range, and the cook and the one remaining hand were occupied around the ranch buildings.

His wife had told him on his return that she, with their twenty-year-old daughter Miriam and their second child, a ten-year-old boy called Joey, were inside the house when a bunch of seven riders, all strangers, approached the ranch buildings.

The man riding at the head of the group was tall and thin, with a long, cruel face, scarred down one cheek, and a cold eye to match. His companions were a similarly unpleasant-looking lot. All were armed with rifles and revolvers. Their clothing was dirty and travel-stained.

Ranger's wife had spotted the approaching riders through a window. Apprehensive, she looked towards the cook and the ranch hand who were standing outside the barn, closely watching the strangers riding in. Suddenly, the two men turned and ran towards the bunkhouse, where some weapons were kept. The leader of the riders spoke to a man just behind him, who quickly turned his horse and chased after the two running men.

Leaping from his horse as he came up to the bunkhouse the man ran to the door, drawing his gun, and ran inside, close behind the two men. A moment later, Emily Ranger heard the sound of a gun being fired twice, and shortly after this the stranger came out of the bunkhouse, mounted his horse and rode back to his companions, who had now reached the house and were dismounting.

Mrs Ranger had told her son to run upstairs and hide inside a big empty chest standing in his bedroom. Then, after dropping a stout wooden bar in position to hold the outside door closed, she and her daughter ran to an open-fronted cupboard standing against the wall, in which two Winchester rifles were resting.

As they each grabbed one of the rifles, they heard a violent hammering on the door. Mrs Ranger knew the rifles were always left unloaded and she looked around for the ammunition. She spotted the box on a shelf just out of reach of both her and her daughter.

She ran for a chair on which to stand in order to reach the ammunition, but before she could carry it back to the cupboard, the door gave way under a massive impact and a big, heavily built man, with a slight cast in one eye, hurtled into the room and fell on the floor on top of the door.

He was followed by the leader of the group and another of his men. They ran up to the two women and wrested the rifles from them. While they were doing this, Miriam pulled the leader's gun from its holster, but before she could turn it on him he struck her savagely on the side of the head with the rifle butt and she collapsed on the floor. Mrs Ranger knelt down beside her daughter.

The leader had then looked into the bedroom downstairs used by Ranger and his wife, only to find it empty. He went upstairs and shortly after he came down with Joey. His men tied the two women hand and foot. Miriam was still unconscious. The leader placed a sheet of paper on the table and he and his men rode off with the boy.

'When I got back with my hands a couple of hours after the men left,' said Ranger, 'Miriam had come round. We freed her and her mother, then went over to the bunkhouse. The cook and the ranch hand I'd left behind were inside. Both men were dead, shot through the head.'

He took a folded sheet of paper from his pocket and handed it to Jim. 'You'd better read this,' he said.

Jim unfolded the sheet and studied the message, in rough capital lettering, which had been scrawled upon it.

It read: SEND ONE OF YOUR HANDS ALONE AND UNARMED TO DIABLO CANYON AT NOON THREE DAYS FROM TODAY WITH 20 THOUSAND DOLLARS IN BANKNOTES AND THE BOY WILL BE HANDED OVER. IF THE MONEY DONT TURN UP OR YOU BRING THE LAW IN THE BOY DIES.

'So you haven't brought the law in?' asked Jim.

'How could I?' groaned Ranger. 'When Joey's life's at stake. In any case, the nearest lawman's sixty miles from here. And another thing, we couldn't report the killings of the cook and the other hand. As it happens, neither of them has any kin. We buried them both on the far side of the corral.'

'About the money?' asked Jim. 'They've given you three days to get it. Is there any problem about getting it in time?'

'No,' replied Ranger. 'Six months ago my father died back East and left me a sizeable chunk of money – more than what they're asking for. I figure maybe the kidnappers know about that. I can pick up what's needed at the bank in Linford tomorrow. That's a town five miles north of here.'

Jim asked Mrs Ranger if she could give a closer description of the men who had burst into the house.

'The two I remember best,' she said, 'are the leader and the big man who smashed the door down.' She proceeded to give Jim a detailed description of the two.

Jim spoke when she had finished. 'I'm pretty

sure I know who those two are,' he said. 'I saw them on a Wanted poster when I was a sheriff in Colorado. They sound very much like a man called Josh Vickery, who leads a gang of outlaws, and his *segundo*, a man called Barton. They've robbed trains, stagecoaches and banks, and they were suspected of stealing cattle as well. It looks like they've added kidnapping to their list of easy ways to make money. Up to now, they've operated mostly in Kansas.

'A friend of mine,' he went on, 'actually witnessed Vickery and three other members of the gang robbing a bank in Wichita five months ago, when a deputy marshal was killed. Vickery's mask slipped and he was recognized.'

'I've *got* to send the money the day after tomorrow,' said Ranger. 'You can see that, can't you?'

'Yes,' agreed Jim. 'You ain't got no choice. There's a good chance they won't harm the boy so long as you hand the money over and don't bring the law in.'

'I'd like to take the money myself,' said Ranger, 'but I can't ride a horse and I'd never make it on a buckboard. And in any case, that message says that one of my hands has to take it.'

'I'd like to take the money for you,' said Jim. 'They ain't to know that I'm not one of your hands.'

'We're mighty grateful for the offer,' said Ranger. 'My men are all pretty good at handling cows, but delivering a kidnap ransom is a bit out of their line, and I haven't talked it over with them yet.'

'That's settled, then,' said Jim. 'Just where is this Diablo Canyon?'

'Ten miles north-west of here,' replied Ranger. 'You can't miss it. It's a deep, narrow gorge, dry and steep-walled, closed at one end, with a flat-topped mesa half a mile to the west of it. I'll give you directions on the best way to get there.'

'Poor Joey,' said Mrs Ranger. 'He must be half-scared to death. How can people sink so low as to take a young boy like that away from his parents? You don't reckon they'll harm him, do you, Mr Cochrane?'

'Not so long as they get the money,' replied Jim. 'There'd be no reason to hurt him then. He should be home again in a couple of days.'

'I sure hope so,' she said. 'We'll all be worried sick till he gets back.

'We've got a spare room upstairs you can sleep in,' she went on. 'We can bring a spare bunk over from the bunkhouse. I'll get two of the hands to do that right now. And there'll be some supper on the go in about an hour.'

When Jim went down from his room into the living-room forty minutes later, Ranger was sitting in his armchair talking to a young woman whom Jim took to be his daughter Miriam. She was a slim attractive girl, with light-brown hair and her mother's good looks. An angry-looking bruise discoloured the whole of the left side of her face. Her father introduced her to Jim.

'Pardon my looks, Mr Cochrane,' she said. 'I think you know what happened to my face. Father's told me that you're going to help us out.'

'I'll do what I can to get your brother back,' said Jim. 'And maybe, after that, I can help to put the gang where they belong. They shouldn't be allowed to get away with what they're doing.'

During the following conversation, while awaiting Mrs Ranger's call to supper, Ranger told Jim that there was just a faint possibility – no more than that – of him regaining the normal use of his legs at some time in the future. 'It could happen anytime,' he said, 'or it could never happen at all.'

On the following afternoon the rancher went into Linford on the buckboard to collect the ransom money. Jim accompanied him, helping him on and off the buckboard.

The rest of the day passed slowly, and Jim could sense the mounting anxiety of the Rangers as they waited to be reunited with Joey.

TWO

Jim set out after breakfast the following morning, timing his departure so as to arrive at Diablo Canyon around noon. Silently, the Rangers watched him go, then went inside to begin the long agonizing wait until his return.

Jim followed the route described by Ranger, and half an hour before noon he spotted in the distance the top of the mesa which stood in the vicinity of Diablo Canyon. He had seen no riders on the way. He rode towards the mesa, and soon the lower end of Diablo Canyon came into view. He paused for a moment, looking towards it, but there were no signs of any human presence, and he thought it likely that the outlaws would be watching him from some vantage point nearby, to make sure he was alone.

Before continuing, he looked around and stiffened when he saw a bunch of riders, eight in all, coming towards him from the west. He hesitated, then decided to stay where he was until the approaching riders reached him.

His first thought was that they were members of the gang coming to relieve him of the ransom money. But there was no sign of a boy with them. Then, as they drew closer, he realized with dismay that they were a band of Texas Rangers.

When the riders reached Jim, Ranger Foster, the one in the lead, gave the signal to stop. He looked closely at Jim, then spoke to him. At the same moment a man lying on top of the distant mesa, who had been watching Jim and the posse through field-glasses, hurriedly left his position and started climbing down the far side of the mesa.

A quarter of the way down, he stopped and signalled, by waving his arms, to another man on a piece of high ground to the north. Then he continued his hurried descent, mounted his horse at the foot of the slope, and rode off fast to the north.

'Where've you come from, stranger?' Foster asked Jim.

Jim thought quickly. He figured it was probable that his chance meeting with the posse had been seen by the outlaws, and if that was so, they would be hightailing it out of the area by now, either taking the boy with them or leaving his dead body behind.

But he couldn't be sure of this. And the posse was riding in a direction which would keep it well clear of Diablo Canyon. He decided to carry on with his original plan.

'From Amarillo,' he replied. 'I'm heading for my father's ranch in Colorado.'

'We're chasing three men,' said Foster. 'Happen you've seen them? They've been rustling cattle on the New Mexico border. There's two white men and one half-breed. The 'breed's riding a pinto.'

'Sorry, I can't help you,' said Jim. 'I ain't seen a soul since I broke camp this morning.'

'We lost their tracks a while back,' said Foster, 'but we reckon they're heading east for The Nations. We'll be on our way.'

As they rode off Jim turned his horse and headed for the canyon, fearing the worst. When he reached the entrance he rode through it, then along the floor of the canyon for its full length of half a mile. It was deserted.

He waited in the canyon until two hours after noon, then, convinced that the kidnappers had departed, he rode to the mesa, climbed to the top and searched it. He found signs that someone, probably a look-out, had recently been stationed there. He returned to the foot of the mesa, and searching the area to the north he came across a small ravine where a number of men had recently been camping. Carefully, he inspected the signs they had left behind them, and finally he saw what he had been looking for.

It was the clear imprint left by a boot so small that it could only have been worn by a young boy or girl. He could only make a rough guess at the number of men who had been there. At least six, he thought. There were signs of a hurried departure.

Making the best time possible, Jim rode back to the Diamond R, dreading the task of telling the rancher and his family why he was returning alone. As he approached the house, the rancher and his wife and daughter came out and awaited his arrival. There was a look of despair on their faces.

Quickly, Jim explained what had happened. He said he was sure that the outlaws had spotted him with the posse and had jumped to the conclusion that the law had been brought in to free the kidnapped boy. As Jim finished, Mrs Ranger, distraught, asked the question which was in all their minds.

'D'you think, Mr Cochrane, that this means that they will have killed Joey?'

'I honestly can't say,' replied Jim. 'I saw his footprint in the ravine where the outlaws were hiding, and it looked like they'd taken him with them. What they might do is to hold on to him for a while, with the idea of trying for the ransom money again, later on. I reckon they're well away from here by now, after seeing that posse.'

'Poor Joey,' she said, despairingly. 'So there's nothing we can do about it, except wait, and hope that he's still alive?'

'I don't see it that way,' said Jim. 'I'd like to see if I can pick up the trail of the gang, and if I find them and Joey's still with them, I'll do my best to set him free and bring him back here. But it's up to you to decide.'

They stared at him, worry and indecision on their faces. Then the rancher spoke.

'If you were in my place what would *your* answer be?' he asked.

'I'd agree with what I've just suggested,' Jim replied. 'I'd want to get the boy away from the gang just as soon as I could. Now that they think there's a posse after them, they won't be expecting to be followed by just one man. That'll give me an edge over them, I reckon.'

'However you look at it,' said the rancher, 'it's a mighty brave thing for you to offer to do for us.'

'No braver than what you did for my father during the war,' said Jim.

Ranger looked at his wife. 'What d'you think, Emily?' he asked.

'I think Mr Cochrane's right,' she replied. 'If Joey's still alive, I want him back here before any real harm comes to him. So I'm mighty grateful to Mr Cochrane for offering to risk his own life to help us.'

'I feel the same way,' said the rancher. 'When will you leave?'

'Right now,' said Jim, 'while their tracks are still fresh. But I'd better have a change of clothes and a different horse, just so's the outlaws don't recognize me as the man they saw talking to the posse when they were spying on us from the top of that mesa.'

'I'll get some of Will's clothes for you,' said Mrs Ranger. 'They should fit you well enough.'

'Miriam,' said the rancher, 'run out and tell Buck to pick out a good horse and slap Mr Cochrane's saddle on it. Tell him to pick out a horse that ain't anything like the one Mr Cochrane's been riding.'

'Thanks,' said Jim. 'Is Joey a good rider?'

'Pretty good,' replied Ranger. 'He likes horses. Started riding as soon as he could stay on a saddle.'

Jim left half an hour later, carrying provisions and a bedroll with him. The rancher, his wife and daughter by his side, stood and watched him go. Then Miriam called out and ran after him.

'Mr Cochrane,' she said. 'You know that Joey means everything to the three of us and if you bring him back we'll always be in your debt. But the men who took him are evil men. Please take care of yourself.'

'I'll do that,' said Jim, 'and I'm looking forward to seeing a lot more of you when I get back with Joey.'

She blushed, and ran back to her parents, and all three stood looking after Jim, in silence, until he passed out of sight. Then, with heavy hearts, they walked back into the house.

Jim headed for the ravine in which he had found the outlaws' camp. It was dark when he arrived and he spent the night there.

At daylight, he looked closely at the prints left

by the horses' shoes. Although not an experienced tracker, he had benefited considerably from the expertise displayed by Fred Sibley, a white ex-Army scout and mountain man, who had settled in Colorado when he retired. Sibley had helped Jim on a number of criminal-chasing expeditions and Jim, who had been impressed by his tracking abilities, had closely observed his technique.

The tracks leaving the camp led eastward and Jim followed them until nightfall. He could see that the outlaws had been moving at a fast pace. He camped for the night in a shallow draw and resumed his pursuit at sunrise, keeping a close watch ahead for any sign of the men he was following, and scanning the ground for tracks as he rode along in an eastward direction.

In the afternoon he reached the spot, in a small hollow, where the outlaws had camped the previous night and he breathed a sigh of relief as, once again, he spotted a print of Joey's boot, confirming that the boy had still been alive the night before.

Jim carried on until nightfall, as quickly as he was able. Occasionally he lost the tracks, but always managed to pick them up again later on. There had been no change in their direction during the day. On the following day, setting off at dawn, he proceeded in the same way, and in the afternoon he reached the place where the outlaws had camped the previous night. Once again he saw signs of Joey's presence there.

On the following day, when he judged that he

was in Indian Territory, not far behind the outlaws, he noticed that one of the riders he was following had left the main party, to ride off in a north-easterly direction. The rest of the party had continued on as before. Jim hesitated for a moment, then decided to follow the main body of the party.

Ten miles further on he heard gunfire ahead, which continued as he rode up to a small hill directly in his path. Riding round the base of the hill he stopped when he saw, two hundred yards ahead, a horse lying motionless on the ground, with a white man lying against it.

Two mounted Comanche braves were circling the horse, firing their rifles at the man against it. He was returning their fire, using his horse as a shield as best he could.

Before the Indians had spotted him, Jim rode back behind the hill, dismounted, and carrying his Winchester rifle he crawled around the base until he could see the two braves again. Then, lying on the ground, he started firing at the two moving targets. His second shot hit one of the braves in the shoulder. The Indian jerked backwards, then yelled to his companion, and they both wheeled their mounts and galloped off to the south.

Jim ran back to his horse, mounted it, and rode towards the man and horse on the ground, holding his rifle up in the air as he did so. As he drew closer, he could see that the man was tall, bearded

and heavily built. Then, as he saw the slight cast
in one eye and remembered Mrs Ranger's description of the man who had battered down the door
of the ranch house, he became convinced that he
was looking at Barton, Vickery's *segundo*.

He could hardly believe his luck. There was a
real chance now, he thought, of discovering the
whereabouts of the rest of the gang and Joey.

'You all right?' he asked as he rode up to Barton
and dismounted.

'My leg's broken,' groaned Barton. 'One of them
Indians shot my horse down and it rolled over me
after it fell.'

Jim glanced at the horse. It was dead, shot
through the head. Then he bent over Barton, who
was lying propped up on his elbow, with one hand
holding the upper part of his leg.

'You figure the bone's broken there?' asked Jim.

'I'm sure of it,' said the outlaw. 'I can feel the
bone grating under the skin.'

'I'd best get splints on it, then,' said Jim. 'Is
there a doctor anywhere near here?'

'Not that I knows of,' replied Barton, 'but I've
got some friends five or six miles east of here. I
left them a while back to call in at a small settle-
ment north-west of here and I was on my way to
join up with them again when them two Indians
showed up. One of them helped an Army doctor
for a few years. He'll know how to put this leg
right.'

'Have they got a buckboard there?' asked Jim.

'No, they ain't,' said Barton.

'One thing's sure,' said Jim. 'With that leg like it is, you can't ride a horse without doing it a lot more damage. I'm going to have to build a travois.'

He pointed to a small stand of trees some four hundred yards away. 'I'll ride down there for some timber,' he said. 'You stay here and don't move.'

With only his 10-inch Bowie knife to help him, it took Jim over an hour to cut two splints, the two long shafts for the travois and sufficient crosspoles to form a platform which would accommodate Barton's large frame. He tied all the items together with his lariat, mounted his horse and dragged the bundle behind him to where Barton was lying.

He untied the bundle, picked out the two splints, and using some rope he lashed them tightly in position, one on each side of the outlaw's leg. Then he constructed the travois, using his own rope and Barton's to lash the crosspieces to the two long shafts.

Finally, he crossed the front ends of the two shafts and lashed them together. Then he lifted them so that the crossover point was above his horse's head and a shaft ran down each flank of the animal.

'I reckon that'll do,' he said.

Barton grunted, then grimaced with pain.

'Where were you heading when you turned up here?' he asked.

'I've been punching cows in the Texas Panhandle,'

Jim replied. 'I was heading for Ellsworth. My folks run a homestead near there. My name's Jim Cochrane.

'Let's get you on this travois,' he went on. 'The sooner you get to your friends, the better.'

Barton, with a volley of curses and agonized groans, climbed, with Jim's help, on to the travois and Jim, using the reins from the outlaw's horse, lashed him into position to prevent him sliding off the platform.

Then he took the reins of his horse and headed slowly in the direction indicated to him by Barton. As far as possible, and against his inclination, he led his horse over smooth ground to make the journey less painful for the outlaw.

After they had been travelling for just under two hours, Barton shouted to Jim to watch out for a flat-topped hill, and beyond that a grove of trees adjacent to a stream. His friends, he said, would be inside the grove. Twenty minutes later, Jim rode around the base of the hill and headed for the grove, about four hundred yards ahead.

THREE

As Jim approached the trees, two men holding rifles stepped out into the open. Jim stopped in front of them. One of the men kept his rifle pointed at Jim, while the other walked past him to see who was on the travois. His eyes widened as he looked into the grim face of Barton, then at the splints on his leg. He called out to the man who was holding his rifle on Jim.

'Go and bring Ben Gardner,' he said. 'Tell him Brad's turned up with a broken leg.'

As the man left, Jim walked back to stand beside Barton. He started to undo the ties holding him on the travois platform. A moment later, Ben Gardner and Vickery, the gang leader, came running out of the trees. They both took a close look at Jim. Then Gardner turned his attention to Barton's broken leg. After a quick examination, he glanced at Jim.

'You done a good splinting job there,' he said. 'Now we'd better carry him to one of the tents. Two on each side, careful-like.'

'This is Jim Cochrane,' said Barton. 'If he hadn't happened by when a couple of Comanches shot my horse down, I'd likely be dead meat by now. He turned up just when I was running out of ammunition.'

Jim helped the other three to carry Barton through the trees to a clearing in the centre of the grove where six Army-style officers' tents had been pitched. Three other men awaiting them in the clearing walked up to have a look at Barton as he was carried into one of the tents. Jim noticed that one of the three appeared to be barely out of his teens.

Inside the tent, they laid the injured outlaw on the ground. Then Vickery turned to Jim. 'I'll see you outside in a few minutes, Cochrane,' he said. 'I'd like a few words with you.'

As Jim left, Vickery spoke to the man who had helped himself, Jim and Gardner to carry Barton inside. 'Keep a close eye on Cochrane,' he said, 'and don't let him leave. I'll be out soon.'

When Jim left the tent he walked a few paces away from it, then stopped and looked around. There was no sign of Joey, but he could be in any one of the other five tents. A camp-fire was burning in the centre of the clearing. Around it, three men were sitting.

Until Vickery came out of the tent fifteen minutes later, Jim chatted with the man who had left the tent close behind him. As Vickery approached them the man left Jim and walked

towards the three men sitting around the camp-
fire. Vickery spoke to Jim.

'You told Barton you were a cowpuncher,' he
said, 'but you don't look like one to me.'

'It so happens I ain't,' said Jim. 'I'm running
from the law. I'm telling you this because I've just
figured out who you are. I was standing just across
the street from that bank you robbed in Wichita
about five months ago. A deputy marshal was shot
down when you were leaving. Your own mask
slipped and me and a few others saw your face.'

Startled, Vickery looked uncertainly at Jim. His
hand moved close to the handle of his Colt .45.

'You say the law's after you?' he said.

'That's right,' replied Jim. 'About six months
ago I got tired of being honest and I robbed a
couple of small banks in the New Mexico
Territory. But the Rangers got on to my trail, so I
headed for Indian Territory to lie low there for a
while.

'I can't say that I really took to working on my
own. Lonely and dangerous is what it was and not
much to show for the risks I was taking. I was
wondering if maybe I could join up with you.'

Vickery pondered for a moment, closely studying Jim's face. Then he replied.

'I could do with another man,' he said. 'I've got
a big job coming up in a few weeks' time. And you
did us a favour when you stopped those
Comanche braves from lifting Barton's scalp. I'll
take you on and we'll see what you're made of.'

He pointed to a tent on the other side of the fire. 'Use that tent over there,' he said. 'Nobody else is using it right now. But first, come and meet the others.'

With Jim by his side he walked over to the four men by the fire.

'This is Jim Cochrane,' he said. 'Seems he's an outlaw like ourselves. Says he'd like to join the gang, so I'm going to give him a try. You all know what he did for Brad.'

He turned to Jim.

'That's my nephew Earl over there,' he said, pointing to the one who looked barely out of his teens, 'and on his right is Joe Hines, then Mark Catt and Sid Bellamy.'

Jim nodded at the men, then sat down on the ground beside them as Vickery returned to the tent into which Barton had been taken.

The four outlaws were obviously curious about Jim, and drawing on his imagination he talked about the two bank robberies he had mentioned to Vickery. He told them that the two robberies had yielded no more than $200 or so.

'It was hardly worth the risk,' he said.

'What's needed,' said Earl Vickery, disparagingly, 'is a brain behind the operation. Take my uncle, for example. All our robberies are properly planned and we don't do any job that ain't worth our while and that carries too much risk of our getting caught. That's why none of us has ever been taken by the law yet.'

'I sure was lucky to meet up with you men,' said Jim. 'I can't wait for your next job to come along.'

Shortly afterwards, as darkness was falling, Hines and Catt got up to prepare supper and Jim continued to chat with Vickery's nephew and Bellamy. It was clear, from his patronizing manner, that Earl Vickery had a very high opinion of himself.

When supper was ready, Josh Vickery and Gardner were still in the tent with Barton. Hines took plates of food along to them, while Jim and the others went to collect their own plates from Catt and sat down close to the fire to eat.

Catt put some food on an empty plate.

'I'll take this to the boy,' he said to Hines, and walked over to a tent near to the one which Jim had been told to use.

Jim sighed inwardly with relief. Then he raised his eyebrows in simulated surprise. Earl Vickery smiled condescendingly at him.

'Robbing banks and trains and stagecoaches ain't the only way we make our money,' he said. 'There's a young boy in the tent there, pining for his folks. When the time's right my uncle aims to hand him back to them in exchange for a sizeable chunk of ransom money.'

Jim looked at him admiringly. 'I sure have ended up with the right sort of people,' he said. 'You got another job in mind just now?'

'Soon maybe,' said Earl Vickery. 'Just now, we're resting up here for a short spell.'

After supper, Josh Vickery and Gardner came over to join Jim and the others. The outlaw leader told them that Barton's leg should heal up without any complications, but he'd have to rest up for quite a while. He told Jim that a guard was posted over the camp every night, relieved every three hours, and that he would have to take his turn the following night.

After a spell of desultory conversation the men started to turn in at around ten o'clock. Gardner went to the tent where Barton was lying. The two Vickerys went to another tent, Hines and Catt to another. Bellamy went to the tent in which Jim now knew that Joey was being held.

Jim walked over to the picket line, near the edge of the clearing, where his horse was tied, and picked up his saddle-bags and rifle, which were lying on the ground with his saddle. He noticed that the horses were picketed in two groups, a few yards apart. His own was in a group of three, the other group contained six.

As Jim turned to walk over to the tent he was to occupy, Hines left the tent he was sharing with Catt and walked over to a large boulder standing near the edge of the clearing. He was carrying a rifle and wearing a six-shooter. He sat down with his back against the boulder, clearly on duty as a night guard. Presumably, he would be relieved in three hours' time.

The night was sultry and as Jim reached his tent he turned and looked to the east where it looked like some storm clouds were forming. He turned, lifted the tent flap, and went inside. He lit the oil lamp hanging from the tent pole. There were two roughly built bunks inside.

He sat on one of the bunks and considered the situation. He decided that he had better make his move to rescue Joey soon after the guard changed at around one o'clock in the morning. He extinguished the lamp, then lay down on the bunk and tried to relax.

Just before one o'clock he walked up to the tent flaps and looked through a gap at Hines, sitting against the boulder. Five minutes passed, then Hines stood up and walked back to his tent. A few minutes later Catt left the tent, threw more wood on the fire, and took up the position against the boulder recently vacated by Hines. Jim's tent was not in front of him, but to one side.

Jim waited for half an hour, then checked that he had his knife and Peacemaker. He took from a saddle-bag a long piece of strong cord and stuffed it in his pocket. Then, with his knife, he cut a long slit in the wall of the tent remote from the guard, picked up his rifle and eased his way out. As he did so he could see a faint light showing from inside the tent where Joey was held prisoner.

He paused, then crouched and moved silently towards the edge of the clearing. Glancing towards the boulder he could see Catt sitting there, motionless. When he reached the shelter of the trees he circled around until he was close to

Catt and paused as the outlaw coughed and
moved his head. He waited a short while, then
took out his knife, placed his rifle on the ground
and moved around a little further until he was
abreast of the outlaw and only a few yards away
from him.

As he took a step towards Catt a dry twig
snapped under his foot. The outlaw rose and
turned to face Jim, drawing his six-shooter as he
did so. But before he had levelled and cocked it,
the sharp point of Jim's knife, thrown with force
and unerring accuracy, had entered his chest and
penetrated his heart. He staggered backwards
and collapsed on the ground.

Jim went up to him to retrieve his knife, and to
place the body in a sitting position against the
boulder. Then, carrying his own rifle and Catt's,
he walked through the trees to where his horse
was tethered. On the way, he heard a faint rumble
of thunder in the distance.

Reaching his horse he located his saddle and
bridle close by, and working in the semi-darkness
he saddled the horse and put the bridle on. He did
the same for the horse, a smaller one, which was
standing next to his. He slid a rifle into the saddle
holster on each mount, then led both horses
through the trees and tied them securely to a tree
on the boundary of the grove.

Holding his Peacemaker he circled round
through the trees to a point closest to the tent
containing Bellamy and Joey. He walked up to the

tent from the rear and saw that there was still a faint light coming from inside. He listened for a few moments and thought he could hear a faint snore inside. Then, once again, he heard a rumble of thunder, nearer this time.

He walked round to the front of the tent and keeping his voice down he spoke through a narrow gap between the tent flaps.

'Sid,' he called out hoarsely, repeating the call until Bellamy woke and replied.

'What's up?' he asked. 'And who's that?'

'It's Mark,' replied Jim, in a low voice. 'Come out and give me a hand. There's something out there scaring the horses. I'll go and get Joe to give a hand as well.'

Still half asleep, Bellamy cursed, and a couple of minutes later he opened the tent flaps and came out, with his head bent forward. Jim, waiting outside, struck the outlaw over the head with the barrel of his Peacemaker, dragged him, unconscious, inside the tent and closed the flaps. As he did so, a blinding flash of lightning illuminated the camp, followed immediately by a deafening crack of thunder from above.

Jim looked round inside the tent. On a bunk at the back Joey was lying, fully dressed except for his boots, staring at Jim. His hands and feet were tied. Jim took the cord from his pocket and hog-tied Bellamy, then used the outlaw's bandanna to gag him. He walked over to the boy.

'I'm Jim Cochrane, Joey,' he whispered. 'I've

come from your father. I'm taking you back home.'

He cut through the ropes holding the boy's wrists and ankles together.

'I've got two horses ready for us outside, Joey,' he said. 'Put your boots on and we'll leave.'

Glancing down at Bellamy Jim could see that the outlaw had come to.

Joey hastily put his boots on and stuffed his red bandanna, a present from his sister, in his vest pocket. Jim opened the flaps and stepped outside, with Joey close behind. Looking towards the horses at the picket lines, Jim could see that one of the trees behind them was on fire. It had obviously been struck by lightning. He could see that the animals were getting restive.

'Follow me, Joey,' he said, 'and keep close.'

As he moved off, heading for the nearest trees, there was another vivid flash of lightning and he saw Hines standing outside his tent. At the same moment Hines saw Jim and the boy. There was another flash of lightning and Jim and Hines fired simultaneously at one another.

The shot from Hines missed its target, but the bullet from Jim's Peacemaker lodged in the outlaw's right arm. At the sound of the shots the other outlaws spilled out from their tents, but by the time the next lightning flash came, Jim and the boy had disappeared into the trees.

Jim had originally intended to untie the horses on the two picket lines and chase them off, in order to delay pursuit by the outlaws. But there was now no time to do this. He headed for the two mounts he had saddled earlier.

Following Jim, a few feet behind him, Joey suddenly tripped and fell. His shout to Jim was drowned by a clap of thunder, and when he climbed to his feet, Jim was out of sight. He stood, scared, wondering which direction to take. When he did move, it was in a direction at a slight angle to that taken by Jim.

When Jim realized that Joey was not behind him he started a frantic search for the boy, calling out his name. It was more than a minute before they were reunited. Jim led the way to the horses and they mounted and rode off to the west. As they did so, there was a sudden deluge of rain which extinguished the flames on the burning tree.

Meanwhile, back in the clearing the gang leader shouted orders to his men, and within minutes the two Vickerys, with Bellamy, the latter nursing a sore head, were mounted and heading out of the grove. When they emerged from the trees, the lightning was almost continuous and they caught sight of their quarry just over two hundred yards away. They set off in hot pursuit.

Looking back, Jim saw the following riders and he urged his horse on to a faster pace. Joey followed suit and glancing sideways at him, Jim could see that he was a capable rider.

The rain stopped and the lightning flashes were less frequent now, but they were still of help to the outlaws in following their quarry over the flat ground surrounding the grove. After riding a further mile, Jim looked back, and he could see that the pursuers had lost a little ground.

During the next lightning flash he spotted, on his right, the entrance to a narrow ravine, and calling to Joey to follow, he swung right and headed for it, hoping that he could lose his pursuers by riding into the ravine before the next lightning flash came. But he was unlucky. The flash came just before he and Joey disappeared into the ravine and they were spotted by Earl Vickery, who shouted to his companions and followed the man and boy ahead.

As they rode up the ravine Jim was not sure whether they had succeeded in giving the outlaws the slip. But when they had covered a further quarter of a mile the faint sounds of pursuit from behind told him that they had failed.

They urged their mounts on and raced round a bend in the narrow ravine, but were forced to pull up when they were suddenly confronted with a barrier of earth and loose rocks which stretched across the width of the ravine. It was clear that sometime in the past, a large section of one of the steep high walls had collapsed for some reason and many tons of debris had fallen and blocked the ravine.

Jim could see that it would be impossible for a mounted man to climb over the blockage. He dismounted and pulled his rifle from the saddle holster, telling Joey to do the same. He decided to try and climb out of the ravine and seek a hiding place above.

He called to Joey to follow him, and as he started to clamber up the mound of debris a flicker of lightning showed him that, on the side of the ravine which had collapsed, there was now a much more gradual slope which looked climbable. He headed in that direction, checking occasionally to confirm that Joey was close behind him.

They had started climbing the slope by the time they heard the voices of the outlaws down below.

'Be as quiet as you can, Joey,' said Jim, 'and try not to send any loose stuff rolling down below.'

It was too dark for the outlaws to see them and Jim prayed that the lightning was over.

It was a while before the three outlaws down below, fearing gunfire from Jim, decided on their next move. The two Vickerys started to climb the mound of debris and Bellamy rode back down the ravine, then turned and rode along the top of the wall of the ravine towards the point where it had collapsed.

By the time the Vickerys started climbing, Jim and Joey had reached the top of the slope which led out of the ravine. They ran away from the ravine for about eighty yards until a large patch of dense brush blocked their path. Joey followed Jim into the middle of the patch and they sat down.

'We'll stay here for now, Joey,' said Jim. 'I reckon

we'll be safe here until daylight.' As he finished
speaking they heard the sound of Bellamy's horse
as he rode along the top of the wall of the ravine,
then the sound of voices as he met the two
Vickerys. Soon the sound died away and Jim
spoke to Joey again.

'Did those men hurt you at all, Joey?' he asked.

'Only once,' replied the boy, 'when I tried to get
away. The one called Earl whipped me with a
quirt and said it would be a lot worse if I tried it
again.'

Jim explained to the boy how it came about
that he had come looking for him. He told him
that soon he would be home again with his sister
and parents, and told him to lie down and try to
get some sleep. He himself remained seated,
listening for any sound from the outlaws. Over an
hour passed before he heard the sound of their
voices again nearby. The sound gradually faded
away, then there was silence.

Jim decided that he and the boy would stay
where they were at least until daylight came and
they could see if the outlaws were still around. He
reasoned that Vickery and his men would start
scouring the surrounding country at daybreak,
and being mounted, they would have a big advantage over himself and Joey if he and the boy were
caught out in the open.

When the sun came up, Jim kept watch, peering through the top of the brush. His eye was
caught by something red lying on the ground

about twelve yards outside the boundary of the
brush patch in which they were concealed.
Staring at it, he realized that it was Joey's
bandanna which must have fallen from his pocket
when they were running towards the brush
earlier.

He started moving through the brush, with the
intention of running out to retrieve the bandanna,
but stopped suddenly as he saw a group of three
riders appear on the high ground bordering the
ravine, about three hundred yards away. He
recognized them as the two Vickerys and Bellamy.
They paused for a short while, then split up.

Josh Vickery rode off to the south-west,
Bellamy to the north-west. Earl Vickery headed in
a direction, parallel to the ravine, which would
take him close to the brush in which Jim and Joey
were hiding.

Jim moved to where Joey was lying on the
ground in the middle of the brush. He told him to
stay put and keep quiet, then he crawled back to
the point from which he had been observing the
outlaws. He rose to his feet to look out and see
what Earl Vickery was doing.

The outlaw was riding slowly towards him,
along the top of the wall of the ravine. As he drew
level, Jim thought for a moment that he was not
going to spot the bandanna. But the outlaw
glanced in his direction, checked his horse, then
turned, rode up to the bandanna, and dismounted
to pick it up.

Looking at the bandanna, Vickery recognized it as Joey's. He looked across at the brush and lifted his six-gun from its holster. He hesitated, then walked directly towards the point from which Jim was observing him.

Jim, peering through the top of the brush, could have shot Vickery down before he came any closer, but he knew that the sound of gunfire would almost certainly bring the other two outlaws back. He pulled his knife from its sheath, crouched down, and awaited the outlaw's next move.

Vickery paused at the edge of the brush, then started to push through it. Jim, looking along the ground, could see his legs, about twelve feet away, slowly moving directly towards him as the outlaw, his six-gun raised, scanned the top of the brush. When Vickery was within eighteen inches of him, Jim suddenly rose in front of the outlaw, and with his left hand he knocked the gun out of Vickery's hand. A moment later, the knife in his right hand had penetrated the outlaw's heart.

Leaving the dead man on the ground inside the brush, Jim walked up to the outlaw's horse, picked up Joey's bandanna, then called to the boy to come out of the brush and join him. He mounted the horse, then pulled Joey up behind him.

'Everything's all right now, Joey,' he said. 'We'll head east for a while, to keep clear of the two who are looking for us, then we'll strike north for Kansas. Then we'll head for home.'

The following day they crossed into Kansas, and Jim bought a horse and saddle for Joey at a small ranch just over the border. They called in for provisions at a small town three miles west of the ranch and Jim went into a telegraph office to send a message to Joey's parents, telling them that the boy was alive and well, and that they were on their way back from Kansas to the Diamond R, expecting to arrive in five days' time.

FOUR

Four days later, on the Diamond R, Emily Ranger interrupted her chores from time to time to look out of the ranch house windows to the north and north-west for any sign of Joey's return. But it was not until the following day, late in the afternoon, that she spotted two riders, one small enough to be a boy, moving fast towards the ranch house.

Excitedly, she called out to her husband and Miriam, and all three of them went outside to await the arrival of the two riders. Soon they could identify them as Jim and Joey and they all heaved a sigh of relief.

When the horses stopped in front of them Joey dismounted and ran over to his mother, who, sobbing with relief, embraced him. Then his father and sister both hugged him. When the joy of reunion had abated a little, Ranger, his wife beside him, turned to Jim, who had dismounted.

'This is a great day for us,' he said, 'and all due

45

to you. That was a brave thing you did, going after Joey alone. It's something we'll never forget.'

'I had a fair amount of luck,' said Jim.

'We can hardly wait,' said the rancher, 'to hear exactly what happened since you left us to pick up Joey's trail. Let's all go inside.'

After taking a meal, they all sat down in the living-room and Jim and Joey together gave a full account of their recent experiences. Their audience listened in rapt attention. Then, when the story had been told, Emily Ranger ushered Joey off to bed while Jim continued chatting with Ranger and Miriam.

'I think your father told me once that you'd helped him on the ranch for a spell,' said Ranger to Jim.

'That's right,' replied Jim.

'This job you talked about in the Texas Rangers,' the rancher went on. 'Have you actually joined up yet?'

'Not yet,' replied Jim. 'I figure to do that when I reach Amarillo.'

'The reason I asked,' said Ranger, 'is because I haven't been able to hire more hands since the cook and one of my ranch hands were killed by the Vickery gang. I was wondering if you'd be interested in helping me out here till I can replace them. You'd get foreman's pay for the job, of course.'

Jim looked across at Miriam, who was watching him intently. She nodded her head, then blushed and looked away.

'I'll be glad to help out,' said Jim, 'but there sure ain't no need to pay me.'

'I shouldn't have offered. I'm sorry,' said the embarrassed rancher, hastily. 'You can use the same room upstairs that you used before.'

Things were quiet on the Diamond R for the next few weeks. Jim slipped into the foreman's job without any problems arising, getting on well with the remaining hands and developing a friendship with Miriam. Twice already, greatly enjoying her company, he had gone out riding with her for a couple of hours in the afternoon.

On this particular day he had ridden into Linford alone to buy a few personal items at the store. A man sitting inside the restaurant on the opposite side of the street happened to glance out of the window, and stiffened when he saw Jim dismount, then enter the store.

Hastily, he paid for his unfinished meal, quickly left the restaurant, mounted his horse at the hitching rail outside and rode off fast to the south, on the trail which led to the Diamond R Ranch. He was well out of sight before Jim left the store and walked over to the saloon to quench his thirst.

Twenty minutes later Jim left the saloon, mounted up, and headed for the ranch. As he left town, a distant horseman, who had been watching for him through field-glasses, raced off to the west. Jim was half-way to the ranch buildings when, glancing to his right, he saw smoke rising from the range some distance away.

Surprised, he halted. Although range fires which killed off cattle and burnt off grass on the Texas Panhandle were not unknown during a hot, dry summer, the range at the time was not particularly dry. Seeing that, because of some high ground to the north, the smoke would probably not be visible from the ranch house, he decided to investigate himself.

He rode towards the smoke, and when he drew closer, he could see that it was rising from a small hollow ahead. He headed along the narrow trail towards the rim of the hollow to investigate, but as he skirted a large rock outcrop in his path, three men, without warning, ran out from behind it with drawn guns. The one in the lead ordered him to stop.

It would have been suicide for Jim to draw his Peacemaker. He stopped and rested his right hand on the pommel of his saddle. Shocked, he found himself looking at Josh Vickery, with Gardner and Bellamy both standing beside him. Gardner walked up and took Jim's gun and knife, then returned to stand by Vickery, who ordered Jim to dismount. Jim did so, and stood by his horse. Grim-faced, Vickery looked at him.

'You didn't think you'd get away with it after killing two of my men, did you, Cochrane?' he asked. 'We figured maybe we'd find you here.

'There are two things we aim to do,' he went on. 'First, we're taking you to see my brother Brett.

He's Earl's father, and he can't wait to get his hands on the man who killed his only son and left him hidden in a brush patch. It was all of two days before we found him. I was all for finishing you off as soon as we caught you, but Brett begged me to hand you over to him. I've got a feeling that you're going to die real slow and painful-like, Cochrane, once Brett gets his hands on you.'

Grinning, he paused for a moment, visualizing Jim's forthcoming ordeal. Then he continued.

'After we've handed you over to Brett,' he said, 'we're picking up some friends to help us pull off a job in Dodge City. That'll keep us busy for a while, but when it's finished we'll be heading back to the Diamond R to collect that ransom we missed out on a while back. We'll take the boy or the girl – it don't matter which – and we'll ask for twice the ransom we were asking for before.'

He spoke to Gardner and Bellamy. 'Tie his hands,' he said, 'then go and put that fire out before anybody else spots the smoke. I'll watch Cochrane till you get back.'

When the two men returned half an hour later, Vickery ordered Jim to mount his horse and they all headed east, keeping well out of sight of the Diamond R buildings. Two days later they crossed the border into Indian Territory. Although Jim was constantly on the alert to seize any chance of escape, no such chance arose. All three kept watch on him during the daytime, and at night one of the outlaws was always on guard.

They continued in this fashion until, in late afternoon, they reached a narrow, secluded valley located fifty miles into Indian Territory from the Panhandle border. Near a small stream running through the valley were a timber house, several roughly constructed timber buildings and a corral. A small horse herd was grazing on the pasture.

As they rode up to the house a middle-aged man came out, walking with a limp. He bore a strong resemblance to Vickery. He must, thought Jim, be the outlaw's brother, Brett. Two men, Ellery and Newton, walked out of a nearby building and joined him.

As the riders came to a stop outside the house, Brett Vickery, noticing that Jim's hands were tied, stared up at him.

'Is this the man I've been waiting for?' he asked. 'Is this Cochrane?'

'It's Cochrane all right,' his brother replied. 'We brought him back like we promised. He's all yours.'

Brett Vickery regarded Jim with a look of concentrated malevolence. Jim, his face impassive, stared back at him.

'What're you aiming to do with him?' asked Josh Vickery, curiously.

'I ain't finally worked it out yet,' replied his brother, 'but whatever it is, he sure ain't going to like it.'

'I had the idea myself,' said Josh Vickery,

'considering what he done to Earl, that maybe you could hang him upside down and light a fire under his head. A nice, slow-burning fire, that is, so's he wouldn't go too quickly. You wouldn't want him to stop screaming too soon, would you?'

'That's not a bad idea,' said his brother, 'but maybe we can work out something even better. I've got more men coming along to join up with us soon. One of them's a half-Cheyenne called Robert Brand. He lived with the Cheyenne for a few years, and I figure he knows quite a few ways of torturing a man. I'm going to take his advice about what we do to Cochrane.'

Josh Vickery told his brother that he and his men would have to leave as soon as they had taken a meal. Then they dismounted and Jim followed suit. Brett Vickery told Ellery and Newton to take Jim to a small shed behind the house and to tie him up and leave him there.

His brother looked over at the shed. 'You got a good lock on that door?' he asked.

'Ellery fitted one two days ago,' Brett Vickery replied. 'He won't get out of there.'

Newton jammed the muzzle of his six-gun into Jim's back and escorted him to the shed behind the house. Ellery followed behind. Newton pulled back the stout bolt on the door, pushed the door open, and prodded the prisoner inside.

Looking round, Jim was surprised to see a man sitting on the floor in the shed, with his back to the wall. His ankles were bound together and his wrists were tied together in front of him. Around his middle were several turns of rope with the ends tied off on a stout eye-bolt fixed into the wall.

'Meet Deputy US Marshal Dillon,' said Newton. 'He'll be company for you. I figure you two'll have plenty to talk about.'

He searched Jim thoroughly, taking off his gunbelt and throwing it into the corner of the shed. He ordered him to sit down with his back to the wall, facing Dillon. He tied him up in exactly the same way as the deputy marshal had been tied, using a similar eye-bolt in the opposite wall. Then he and Ellery left the shed, bolting the door behind them.

The only light inside the shack came through one small fixed window in the wall to Jim's right. He looked across at the man opposite. An ugly bruise was showing at the top of his temple.

'You all right, Deputy?' he asked.

'Fair,' replied Dillon. 'My head's still pretty sore from a pistol-whipping I got two days ago.'

Jim told the deputy who he was and explained his presence as a prisoner of Vickery's.

'So Josh Vickery's here as well as his brother,' said Dillon. 'We've been after both of them as long as I can remember. We nearly caught Brett three months ago, when we damaged his leg with a rifle bullet. That's why he ain't walking so good. But somehow, he got away.'

'What were you chasing him for?' asked Jim.

'Horse-stealing,' replied Dillon. 'That's what he

specializes in. He got away, but he had to leave the stolen horses behind. He was stealing from over the Kansas border and driving them towards some hiding-place in Indian Territory. We didn't know where that place was at the time.

'Then, a few days ago I started trailing a bunch of stolen horses driven by two men through the Territory. I usually work with a partner, but he was took sick, so I had to do the job alone. I was curious to know where the men were going to hold the horses. I reckon they suspected they were being followed, because one of them back-tracked at night and pistol-whipped me. Then they brought me here with them.

'I was surprised to find Brett Vickery here when we arrived,' he continued. 'I had no idea it was his men I was following.'

'D'you know what he aims to do with you?' asked Jim.

'I do,' replied Dillon. 'He told me. He weren't too pleased at being crippled by a lawman, and he's planning to have his men take me a long way from here, then finish me off and leave my body lying somewhere where it's bound to be found right away. He don't want to risk a bunch of deputies being sent out to search for me when I don't turn up. How about you?'

'Well,' said Jim, 'like I told you, I killed his son Earl, so he don't want me to die easy. I'm waiting to find out what he has in store for me.'

He looked around the shed.

'Do they keep a guard outside this shed at night?' he asked.

'They did for the last two nights,' replied Dillon, 'starting at eight o'clock, with a change of guard about every four hours. They leave a lighted lamp in the shed all night, turned down low. During the day somebody looks in every two hours or so. They let me out, under guard, a few times each day for fifteen minutes or so.'

'It's clear that they don't want to run no risk at all of me getting free. And I reckon they'll feel exactly the same way about you.'

He looked at his bound hands and feet and the rope around his middle securing him tightly to the eye-bolt in the wall.

'I've got to say,' he said, 'that there's no chance at all of us getting free inside here. We can't even help each other to get loose.'

'I wouldn't say that,' said Jim. 'I bought a second-hand belt in a store a couple of months ago and when I started using it I noticed that there was a slit on the inside of the belt at the end away from the buckle. I poked inside with my finger and found a small blade hidden there. It's a thin, flat blade, about an inch and a half long, and razor-sharp on one edge. If I can only get that blade out, maybe I can get my wrists free. But I can tell you, it ain't going to be easy.'

'This is the best news I've heard for a long time,' said the lawman. 'Whoever it was had that belt made, he sure done us a good turn.'

'It was probably some criminal,' said Jim. 'Now tell me, when is the next time somebody's liable to look in on us?'

'They'll be bringing us supper any time now,' replied Dillon, 'and they'll collect the mugs and plates half an hour later. Then the guard will come on at eight, and he'll be relieved at midnight. And when the new guard takes over, he might look in on us.'

'Right,' said Jim. 'I'll start trying to free myself after midnight.'

Supper came shortly after and the utensils were collected half an hour later. A lamp was left burning in the shed. They heard the guard arrive around eight o'clock, and soon after that they heard the sounds of the departing Josh Vickery and his men.

At midnight, there was a change of guard, and the new guard, Ellery, unbolted the door, stepped in and looked around briefly, then left, bolting the door behind him.

Jim started on his bid to free himself and Dillon. He twisted his hands inside the rope and with his right forefinger he felt along the inside of the free end of the belt which had passed through the buckle. He found the slit and tried to insert his forefinger into it, but he found it difficult to twist his hand into the right position, and it was some time before he was successful.

With his finger inside the slit he tried to slide it further in, alongside one of the flat sides of the blade. It was a slow process, but finally he figured his finger had moved far enough along the blade to enable him to ease it out. Slowly and carefully he did this, until finally he was able to grip the blade between thumb and forefinger and pull it free.

He rested for a few minutes, then tried to cut the ropes binding his own wrists together. Finding this impossible, he used the keen blade to saw through the rope holding him to the eyebolt, taking the utmost care not to drop the blade. Then he bent forward to free his ankles, after which he rose and stepped silently over to Dillon. He cut through the rope around the lawman's wrists and handed the blade over to him so that Dillon could first free Jim's wrists, then complete the process of freeing himself.

They froze as they heard the guard outside cough. Then Jim whispered to Dillon.

'We've got to get that man out there to open the door,' he said. 'Then we've got to put him out of action.'

He picked up the longish piece of rope which had been used to secure him to the eye-bolt, and formed a honda and a small loop. At Jim's request, Dillon sat down in his previous position and arranged the cut pieces of rope to give the impression, to the casual eye, that he was still bound.

'Now,' whispered Jim, 'assuming we can get the guard to start opening the door, the first thing he'll see is you. Even if I was sitting where he expects me to be, he wouldn't be able to see me till the door's fully open. When he sees you, I'm counting on him opening the door further to come inside. That's when I'll take care of him.'

'Carry on,' said Dillon. 'It sounds like a good plan to me.'

Jim picked his gunbelt off the floor and buckled it on. He plucked a cartridge out of it, moved over to the door, and started alternately tapping, then scraping, the inside surface of the door with the cartridge, just hard enough to ensure that the noise would be heard by Ellery.

After a short while he stopped, then, a minute later, he started again, a little more vigorously this time. Almost immediately, he heard a noise outside the door, followed by the sound of the bolt being withdrawn.

As the door started to open, Dillon saw Ellery looking in at him, holding a six-gun in his hand. As the outlaw pushed further in, Jim, hiding behind the door, threw his whole weight against it. It smashed against Ellery, trapping him in the aperture. The gun dropped from his hand.

Jim stepped out from behind the door with the rope in his hand, grabbed Ellery, who was in a slightly dazed condition, threw him on the floor face down, and put the loop of rope around his neck. Then, putting one foot on the outlaw's shoulders, he tightened the loop and held it tight until Ellery lost consciousness. Then he loosened it off, picked up the outlaw's gun, and dragged him inside.

Dillon closed the door and expertly bound and gagged the outlaw, who was showing signs of coming to.

'So far, so good,' said Jim. 'Let's leave Ellery here and go after the other two. It's lucky that Josh Vickery and his men left earlier. How d'you reckon we should go about it? I reckon Vickery's in the house and Newton's in that log cabin near the side of the house that I saw him come out of the day they brought me here.'

'That's right,' said Dillon. 'I'm sure that's where they'll be. Let's take them one at a time. It shouldn't be too hard.'

The capture of the two was, in fact, surprisingly easy. First, they located some rope in one of the empty buildings. Then they went for Newton, who woke to find himself looking into the muzzle of a six-gun. He was quickly gagged and tied hand and foot. The same treatment, except for the gagging, was then meted out to Vickery.

Jim and Dillon then dragged Ellery and Newton over to the house to join Vickery, who was almost incoherent with rage. All three were laid down on the floor of the living-room.

Through the remainder of the night, Jim and Dillon each got a little sleep while the other kept guard over the prisoners. In the morning, Jim prepared some food for them all, and when they had eaten, he went outside and had a look round while Dillon guarded the outlaws. He returned a little later and spoke to Dillon.

'What d'you aim to do with these prisoners?' he asked.

'There's a small town called Crispen about twelve miles east of here,' replied Dillon. 'I've been there a few times. That's where I'll take them. I can send a telegraph message for help from there. Maybe they'll send a jail wagon for them.'

'There's a buckboard out there in fair condition,' said Jim. 'How about us slinging those three on to it and taking them to Crispen that way?'

'A good idea,' said Dillon. 'It'll take a bit longer, but it'll be safer and easier than putting them on horses.'

'Right,' said Jim. 'Let's drag them outside where we can see them, then we can go and find our own horses and saddles and a couple of horses to pull the buckboard. But first, I'll see if I can find our weapons.'

He soon found his knife and the two guns in a chest in the living-room. He holstered his own Peacemaker and handed the other six-gun to Dillon. Then they dragged the three outlaws outside.

Half an hour later their horses were saddled and two horses had been hitched to the buckboard. They heaved the three prisoners up on to the floor of the buckboard amid a volley of curses from Vickery and his men. Then they headed for Crispen, with Jim driving the buckboard and his horse tied on behind.

On the way, Jim told Dillon, riding his horse alongside, that he had to move on to Dodge City as soon as he could, in order to catch up with Josh Vickery and his men before they did the job Vickery had talked about. He told Dillon that the outlaw had threatened that when the job was finished they would head for the Diamond R to kidnap Ranger's son or daughter.

He went on to ask the lawman if he would keep the identity of his prisoners secret as long as he could, so as to delay the news of their capture reaching Josh Vickery. If it did, the outlaw would guess that he, Jim, was still alive. Dillon promised to do this.

They reached their destination just after dark and Dillon told Jim to stop outside the livery stable. The owner, Ty Durham, stepped out as they came to a halt. He recognized Dillon as the lawman dismounted.

'Howdy, Deputy,' he said. 'You chasing somebody?'

'The chase is over,' replied Dillon, pointing to the buckboard.

Curious, Durham walked up to it and goggled at the sight of the three bound men lying inside it.

'Horse-thieves,' said Dillon. 'Have you got a room in the stable where I can keep those three till I get some help to take them away for trial?'

'Sure,' said Durham. 'If there's one thing I can't abide, it's horse-thieves. I've got an empty storeroom at the back there that's just right for the job. And there's a cousin of mine who's staying with me just now who used to be a lawman. I know he'd be glad to help you guard these three for a while.'

'I'm obliged,' said Durham, and a few pasers-by stopped and watched curiously as Jim and Dillon pulled the outlaws off the buckboard one by one, and dragged them into the livery stable.

Shortly after this, Jim walked along to the telegraph office and sent a message to Ranger at the Diamond R. It read: *Was captured by Vickery. Now free. Heading for Dodge City after Vickery. He has threatened to kidnap Miriam or Joey. Take all precautions. Jim Cochrane.*

Early the following morning Jim took his leave of Dillon.

'Like I said before, I've got to get to Dodge City as soon as I can,' he explained. 'I want to catch Josh Vickery and his men before they set out for the Diamond R.'

'Go and see Sheriff Miles in Dodge City,' said Dillon. 'He's a good friend of mine, and a good law officer. He used to work with me here in Indian Territory. Tell him about Vickery. I'm sure he'll help you all he can.'

'I'll do that,' said Jim.

FIVE

Two days later, early in the evening, Jim rode into Dodge City and headed for the sheriff's office. There was a light on inside. Sheriff Miles, seated at his desk, looked up as Jim entered. He was a man in his fifties, slim and tall, with a neat moustache and thinning hair.

Jim introduced himself as an ex-lawman in Colorado and told Miles about his recent parting from Deputy US Marshal Dillon and the capture of Brett Vickery and his two men, Ellery and Newton. The sheriff listened with considerable interest.

'Fred Dillon and I were good friends,' he said, 'and I've been wondering how he's been doing. You two did pretty well to capture Vickery and the others. We've been after them for a long time. If only we could capture his brother Josh and his gang as well. Life would sure be a lot easier around here with them out of the way.'

'Maybe we can do just that,' said Jim. He told

the sheriff how he had heard Josh Vickery say,
four days ago, that he and his men were heading
for Dodge to pull off a job there.

Miles sat up. Jim had his full attention. The
sheriff asked whether the outlaw had given any
indication of what the job might be.

'No, he didn't,' Jim replied, 'but he did say he'd
be in this area for a week or two. Has there been
a robbery of any sort around here during the last
two days?'

'No, there ain't,' said Miles, sitting back in his
chair. His brow was furrowed in thought.

'Vickery's had a hand in all sorts of crime,' he
said. 'Stagecoach robbery, train-robbery, bank-
robbery, and even cattle-rustling. Which one is it
this time, I wonder?'

'D'you know of any valuable shipments coming
through by train or stage?' asked Jim.

'No, I don't,' replied the sheriff. 'But I'm going to
check right now with the stagecoach-company
agent and the railway-station manager here. You
like to come along?'

'Sure,' said Jim. 'Maybe I can help you. I'm
mighty keen that Vickery and his men should be
captured while they're around here.' He went on
to tell Miles of the outlaw's threat to kidnap
Ranger's son or daughter on the Diamond R
Ranch in the Texas Panhandle.

Jim left his horse at a livery stable next to the
hotel, then accompanied the sheriff, first to the
stagecoach office, then to the railroad station. But

at each place they drew a blank. No particularly valuable shipments were expected during the next few weeks. They returned to the sheriff's office.

'We know,' said Miles, 'that Vickery's planning is always pretty good. His robberies have all been mighty profitable ones and they've always managed to get clear away afterwards. But this time we've got an advantage over him. We know that he's around, planning something, but he doesn't know that we know.'

'Looks like there's a lot of cattle-drovers and buyers, as well as trail-hands, in Dodge just now,' said Jim.

'That's right,' said Miles. 'We're well into the trail-drive season.'

'Which means,' said Jim, 'that there's an awful lot of money floating around.'

'You're dead right,' said the sheriff, thoughtfully, 'and a lot of it, including all the takings from the saloons and gambling-houses, ends up in that bank you can see a little way down on the other side of the street. I wonder if that's Vickery's target.'

'Could be,' said Jim. 'Has he ever robbed that particular bank before?'

'Not as far as I know,' replied Miles.

'In that case,' said Jim, 'the way he plans his jobs, I reckon he'll want to find out as much as he can about the bank, particularly the layout inside, before he makes his move.'

'You're right,' agreed the sheriff.

'D'you reckon Vickery and his two men Gardner and Bellamy'd be recognized if they came into town?' asked Jim.

'Vickery might be,' Miles replied. 'I've had posters up now and again with his face on them. I don't think he'd risk coming into town himself to look things over. But that wouldn't apply to Gardner and Bellamy.'

'Well,' said Jim. 'I know all three of them pretty well, and I've arrived here not so far behind them, so there's a chance that none of them's been into town yet to look the bank over. What if I hole up in a room in that hotel I noticed opposite the bank? I could watch out for any sign of the gang acting suspicious near the bank. If I spot any of them, we'll know what the target is.'

'I reckon it's worth a try,' said the sheriff. 'I'll take you along to the hotel now. The owner is Grant Farrell. He's a good friend of mine. Better take my field-glasses with you.'

When they went into the hotel, Farrell was standing behind the desk in the lobby.

'Meet a friend of mine, Grant,' said Miles, as he introduced Jim. 'You got a nice room overlooking the street?'

'Sure,' replied Farrell. 'Number three's empty.' He took a key from a hook behind him and handed it to Jim.

'It's likely,' said the sheriff, 'that my friend's going to spend a lot of time in that room for the next few days. But there ain't nothing for you to worry about. He's doing a special job for me. He's looking for somebody, but he don't want to be seen himself.'

'That's all right,' said Farrell, turning to Jim. 'Would you like to take your meals up there? I can fix that with our cook. And if anybody asks, I could say you're resting up after a bad illness.'

'That's a good idea,' said Jim. 'I appreciate the offer.'

Jim and the sheriff went up to Room 3. They walked over to the window. It was directly opposite an alley which ran between the bank and the store.

'This is just right,' said Jim. 'I've got a good view of the front of the bank, and one side as well.'

'I'll leave you now,' said the sheriff. 'I guess you could do with some rest. I'll ask Farrell to send some supper up. I'll come up here to see you some time tomorrow, but if you see anything before then, ask Farrell to send for me.'

After he had taken supper, Jim lay on the bed and slept soundly till morning. After taking breakfast in his room he prepared to keep the bank and its surroundings under surveillance. He pulled a chair up to the window and adjusted the curtains so that he could look through them, unobserved. Then he placed the field-glasses on the window-ledge and sat down.

He watched until dark, eating in his room, without seeing anything suspicious. Sheriff Miles came to see him in the early evening and they talked for a while.

'I was thinking,' said Jim, 'that if I do spot any of the gang looking the bank over, maybe I could follow them when they leave here and find out where they've holed up. If I could get that information for you, maybe you could take a posse out and capture them before they try to rob the bank.'

'I could get a deputy to follow them,' said Miles.

'You're a lawman, and this your territory,' said Jim, 'but I sure would like to trail them myself.'

'In that case,' said Miles. 'I'm going to deputize you for the job. I'd like to surprise them at the hideout because of the risk of people getting killed in town. Let me know as soon as you see any sign of the outlaws.'

Jim saw nothing during the next three days. On the morning of the fifth day of his surveillance, Miles came to his room to see him just after he had finished breakfast. As he stood by the window, looking down into the street, Jim spoke to the sheriff.

'I'm beginning to wonder,' he said, 'whether Vickery's still planning to do a job here. Maybe he's changed his mind for some reason. Maybe he's gone to the Panhandle. I'll stay on watch here till tonight, then I'm heading for the Diamond R.'

He was just turning away from the window when his eye was caught by a horseman approaching slowly along the street below. He stiffened, stared down at the rider, then called out to Miles.

'There's Gardner,' he said.

The sheriff joined him at the window and they both watched as the outlaw rode past the hotel, dismounted outside the livery stable next door, and led his horse inside. He came out shortly after, walked along the boardwalk, and entered the hotel.

'Maybe he's gone into the dining-room,' said Miles, 'or maybe he figured like you did, that this is a good place to watch the bank from, without being seen. Maybe he's taking a room.'

'Let's see if he comes upstairs,' said Jim, opening his door a couple of inches.

A few minutes later they heard footsteps along the passage outside the bedroom doors. Somebody went into the next room and closed the door.

Jim walked over to the window again.

'I'll go down to see Farrell,' said the sheriff. 'I'll find out if Gardner is the man next door. Then I'll have a word with Sam Jordan the liveryman before I come back here.'

As Miles walked towards the door, Jim glanced down into the street.

'Hold it,' he said, looking at a rider who had just come into sight. 'There's Bellamy!'

They watched as Bellamy rode up to the store next to the bank, dismounted, and went inside.

'I'll watch him when he comes out,' said Jim. 'It looks like they're keeping apart while they're in town. You go and find out about Gardner.'

Miles was back in ten minutes. He walked over

to the window to stand by Jim.

'It's Gardner in the room next door,' he said. 'He told Farrell that he was plumb tuckered out and wanted to sleep for a few hours. Said he'd be leaving tomorrow morning. He told the liveryman the same thing. Asked him to have his horse ready at half past nine in the morning. It's clear he'll be watching the bank today. Let's see what Bellamy does when he comes out of the store.'

It was fully twenty minutes before Bellamy appeared, carrying a sack which he tied on to his horse. Then, leaving his mount, he sauntered towards the bank, pausing for a moment to glance along the alley between the bank and the store.

He looked up and down the street, then slipped into the alley. He walked along to the end, then turned and disappeared behind the bank. He reappeared a minute later, walked back along the alley to the street, headed for the door of the bank, and went inside. Fifteen minutes later he left the bank, walked back to his horse, and rode out of town on a trail leading south.

'I'm going out the back way,' said the sheriff, 'and I'm going to find out what Bellamy was doing in the store and the bank. And I ain't forgotten that Gardner'll be watching me from the bedroom next door.'

Jim watched the sheriff go into the store, where he stayed for a short while, then he came out and sauntered along to his office. Ten minutes later he emerged, slowly walked over to the bank and went inside. He reappeared shortly after, stuffing something into his pocket, and walked off down the street until he was out of sight. He quietly entered Jim's room a few minutes later.

'Bellamy bought a sackful of provisions at the store,' he said. 'In the bank, so the cashier told me, he sat down at a table for a while, writing on a piece of paper and looking around occasionally. Then he walked up to the counter and waited his turn behind two other customers. When the cashier was free Bellamy slid a hundred dollar bill across the counter and asked for it to be changed. Then he left the bank.'

'It's clear,' said Jim, 'that they're figuring to rob the bank soon. I'll follow Gardner when he leaves tomorrow. If I find out where they're hiding, can you get a posse together pretty quickly?'

'Sure,' replied the sheriff. 'I'll warn the men I aim to call on that the posse might have to ride at short notice.'

The following morning Jim rose early and, as prearranged with the liveryman, Jordan brought his saddled horse round to the back of the hotel, ready for him to use when Gardner left. It was just after half past nine when Jim, watching from his room, saw Gardner leave the hotel and collect his horse at the livery stable. He rode out of town on the same trail as that followed by Bellamy the previous day.

Fifteen minutes later, Jim went down to his horse, and rode to the outskirts of town, waving to the sheriff as he passed his office. He was just in time to see Gardner disappear from view behind a small distant hill which stood close to the trail he was following. He waited for ten minutes behind a nearby deserted shack, then continued his pursuit of the outlaw.

Exercising the utmost caution to avoid being spotted by Gardner, Jim followed him for seven miles until he reached the beginning of a long stretch of flat ground. From the shelter of a large rock he saw Gardner, well ahead, and now moving in a westerly direction, ride up the side of a long low ridge and disappear from view over its top.

With his field-glasses Jim, from the shelter of the rock, scanned the top of the distant ridge, but could see no signs of movement there. He waited twenty minutes, then scanned the top of the ridge again. He was just about to lower the glasses and continue his pursuit when a flash of reflected light struck his eye, to be repeated a moment later.

Carefully, he looked at the point from which the flash had come and could just make out the figure of a man standing against a boulder perched at the top of the ridge. Then, once again, a flash of light, probably, he thought, reflected from a pair of field-glasses held against the man's eyes, caught his attention.

Jim stayed where he was, watching the top of the ridge. Several times he saw the man slightly change his position. He suspected that the man was acting as a look-out for the Vickery gang, but to confirm his suspicion he would have to get closer.

Since the man on the ridge appeared to have a clear view of the surrounding terrain in all directions, Jim decided that he had better wait until after dark before making any further move. He settled down to wait for nightfall.

SIX

As soon as darkness fell Jim headed for the ridge,
riding under an overcast sky. He headed for a
position at the foot of the slope leading up the
ridge, which was well away from the look-out's
position above. He dismounted and tied his horse
to a small tree at the foot of the slope, then
started the climb to the top of the ridge. The slope
was gradual and, moving as quietly as he could,
he reached the top after climbing steadily for
some twenty minutes.

The ridge was fairly flat across the top, over a
distance of a hundred and thirty yards or so, and
was studded with large boulders. Using these as
cover, Jim made his way slowly towards the spot
where he had seen the look-out standing. He
paused as he heard the faint sounds of voices
ahead of him, seemingly coming from the centre
of the top of the ridge.

He sank down to lie on his stomach, then he
crawled slowly along the ground towards the

sounds, stopping abruptly as he came to the lip of a small hollow on the top of the ridge. Down below, a camp-fire was burning brightly at one side of the hollow and four men were seated around it.

Jim thought he recognized Vickery and Gardner. The other two were strangers to him. They had obviously joined Vickery since he left his brother's horse-ranch for Dodge. He guessed that Bellamy was probably on look-out, somewhere outside the hollow. Five horses were on a picket line well back from the fire.

Jim decided to locate the lookout's position. Slowly, he started to crawl around the rim of the hollow, and soon the flare of a match showed him where the look-out was standing, well back from the rim of the hollow and close to the same large boulder which Jim had seen earlier from a distance.

He crawled round the rim to the point furthest from the look-out and looked down on the four men below. The backs of all four were to him. He decided to move down into the hollow, closer to the men, so that he might hear their conversation. Between him and them were three patches of brush and he figured that in the darkness he could move unseen from one to the other and hide in the patch nearest to them, which was about fourteen feet in diameter.

Fifteen minutes later, he had reached the last patch, and lying on his stomach he wormed his way through, between the stems of the bushes until, peering out from inside the brush, he could see the four seated men. As Jim had suspected, Vickery and Gardner were among the four. The other two were called Slade and Rothery.

They were chatting idly and Jim could only pick out a word here and there. Then, after a while, Gardner rose and walked over to the fire, and from a coffee pot standing there he poured some of the contents into a mug. Then he turned and called out to Vickery.

'What time d'you reckon we should hit that bank in Dodge tomorrow?'

'Right when it opens at ten.' replied Vickery. 'We don't want a lot of people inside when we're robbing it. We'll aim to ride into town just about ten.'

Jim decided to leave as soon as Gardner had returned to sit with the others. He now had all the information he wanted.

But Gardner did not return to the fire. 'I'm going to turn in now, then,' he said, as he drank the coffee.

'Right,' said Vickery. 'I reckon we'll do the same. Don't forget you go on look-out at four in the morning.'

Gardner grunted, and finished his drink.

'I reckon I'll bed down in the same place as I did last night,' he said. 'I dunno how you two can stand Slade's snoring. When he really gets going it sounds like a cattle stampede heading this way.'

He picked up a bedroll, and to Jim's consternation, he headed for the patch of brush in which Jim was hiding. He walked around it, and Jim heard him drop his bedroll on the ground, just outside the brush and against the point where Jim had crawled into it earlier.

A few minutes later, the other three men walked towards Jim, carrying their bedrolls, and dropped them on the ground between him and the fire. The nearest one was not more than seven feet away from him.

Lying motionless in his hiding-place, Jim watched the three men in front of him as they lay down on their bedrolls. He had intended to leave the brush by wriggling backwards along the narrow passage he had made while entering, but this was not now possible, the exit from the passage being blocked by Gardner's bedroll.

Further, he could see that if he attempted to leave the brush at any other point there was a serious danger that the resulting noise and disturbance of the bushes would alert the outlaws to his presence. He decided that there was no option but to stay where he was until Gardner took his turn as look-out.

Jim spent an uncomfortable night, hardly daring to move in his hiding-place. At midnight he saw Bellamy arrive from the look-out point. He woke Slade, who went to take his place.

Four hours later, Slade reappeared and roused Gardner, then went to lie down near Vickery and the others.

Jim gave Slade thirty minutes to settle down, then he inched his way backwards out of the brush, climbed slowly and cautiously out of the hollow, and went along the ridge, then down to his horse. Mounting it, he headed for Dodge, increasing his pace as soon as he judged himself to be out of earshot of Gardner.

He rode into Dodge just as the sun was rising. He went straight to the sheriff's office. Miles was lying on a bunk at the back of the office, fully dressed. He sat up as Jim came in.

'Been waiting here all night for you,' he said. 'What in tarnation happened to you out there?'

Jim explained his late arrival and told Miles that the gang, numbering five, would be riding into town around ten o'clock that morning to rob the bank. 'If we want to catch them all,' he said, 'I reckon that the best place now is here in town, at the bank. If we can surprise them, maybe we can cut down on the gunplay.'

'I think you're right,' said Miles. 'I'm going to round up my deputy and the extra ones I swore in last night. You'd better get something to eat at the hotel, and we'll all meet at the bank in half an hour to work out a plan. We've got plenty of time before Vickery and his men get here.'

Half an hour later, Jim walked over to the bank. Inside were Miles and Denton, his permanent deputy, with four other deputies recently sworn in. The bank president and the cashier were also present.

'Right,' said Miles, as Jim came in. 'Listen up, everybody. I aim to capture these robbers with the least possible risk to ourselves and the bank president and cashier here. The bank door will be open when Vickery and the others arrive, but everything valuable inside will have been moved into the store next door, and there'll be nobody inside the bank.

'I reckon,' he continued, 'that probably Vickery and two of his men will go into the bank and the other two'll stay outside as look-outs. As for us, we'll wait for them in the livery stable opposite the bank. We'll build a barricade inside, close to that big double door. We'll stand behind that.'

He went on to propose that when some of the outlaws had entered the bank, the stable doors should be pushed wide open and the look-outs should be called on to drop their weapons. If they refused, they would be shot down. There was no way out of the bank from the back or sides, and if those outlaws inside came out shooting, they also would be shot down. If they stayed inside, they would be contained in there until they surrendered.

All was ready by 9.30. The townspeople had been warned to stay off the street; the bank door was unlocked, with an OPEN sign showing through a small glass pane; the sheriff and his deputies were standing behind the barricade just inside the stable, with the big double doors closed.

The barricade was set back just sufficiently to

allow the doors to open inwardly. From behind it there would be a good clear view of the whole of the front of the bank when the doors were open.

Outside, the sky was heavily overcast and a blustery wind was picking up dust on the dry surface of the street.

Inside the stable, the sheriff told two of his deputies to stand, one behind each door, ready to pull the door open quickly on his command. Miles himself stood at a small window in the front wall of the stable, watching for the arrival of the outlaws. With his face close to the window, he could see the road coming into town from the south. Jim and the remaining three deputies stood behind the barricade.

'Remember,' Miles ordered the two deputies standing behind the doors, 'don't pull the doors open till I tell you to. When you do, pull them open wide, then get behind the barricade as quick as you can.'

At just three minutes before ten, five riders appeared in view, cantering slowly into town. One of the horses shied as a strong gust of wind blew a cloud of dust into its face. Miles called Jim over.

'Looks like they're here,' he said. 'Are those riders Vickery and his men?'

'No doubt about it,' replied Jim, after a quick look. He returned to his place behind the barricade while Miles continued to watch through the window.

The five riders rode up to the hitching rail

outside the hotel, next door to the livery stable. They dismounted and tied their horses to the rail. Vickery looked up and down the deserted street, then at the OPEN notice on the door of the bank. He and his men crossed the street and stood outside the bank.

Inside the stable Miles spoke to his deputies.

'They're standing outside the bank,' he said. 'Any time now some of them'll be going in. Get ready to pull the doors open when I say so.'

Outside, Vickery was just about to move towards the door of the bank with Gardner and Rothery, when another gust of wind, much more powerful than before, blew across the street directly on to the doors of the stable.

One of the doors was held closed by a deputy, a big man, who was standing close behind it. The other door cannoned into the deputy standing a little way back from it. He was a small man, and the door, its hinges squeaking, sent him reeling backwards as it flew wide open, followed by a cloud of dust which entered the stable.

Miles ran to a position behind the barricade, calling to the big deputy to pull the second door open. But as he reached it, a second powerful gust sent a thick cloud of dust into the faces of the men behind the barricade, temporarily blinding them.

As Vickery and the others heard the stable door fly open, they looked over towards it. Looking through the opening, the outlaw leader stared for a moment in shocked disbelief when he saw the barricade and, through the dust, the heads and shoulders of armed men standing behind it.

He yelled to his men to follow him, then dashed across the street, firing into the stable as he went. His men did the same. They reached the stable before anyone inside was able to fire on them and flattened themselves along the front wall, on one side of the doors.

Three men had been hit by the outlaws' gunfire. Miles and Denton, standing at Jim's side, were both hit, Miles in the head and Denton in the chest. Jim had a bullet-graze, not serious, at the top of his left arm. He and the other two deputies standing close to him were having difficulty in clearing the dust out of their eyes. The two deputies who had been standing behind the doors came and stood behind the barricade looking out into the street.

Jim bent down to look at Miles and Denton. Both men were dead. Grim-faced, he straightened up.

'What do we do now?' asked one of the deputies.

'Stay put, I reckon,' said Jim, 'until we can all see proper. Meantime, watch that door and window. But I don't reckon that Vickery and the others are going to hang around here long.'

Standing against the front wall of the stable with his men, Vickery knew that they would have to leave soon. As he looked towards the open doorway of the stable, his eye was caught by a large oil lamp hanging from a bracket on the wall.

He reached for the lamp, took it down and shook it. He estimated that it was about half full of coal-oil. Quickly, he lit the lamp, moved up towards the doorway and, extending his arm, he flung the lamp over the heads of Jim and the others, towards the middle of the stable. Just as the outlaw released the lamp, he yelled with pain as a bullet from Jim's Peacemaker drilled through his hand. A moment later, the lamp ricocheted off a post set in the floor of the barn and fell on to a pile of hay, the oil spilling out of it. Immediately, the dry hay started burning fiercely.

Jim shouted to two of the deputies to put out the fire. The rest of them stood behind the barricade, ready to repel any attack from outside. When this was not forthcoming, Jim ran to the window, just in time to see the outlaws riding off down the street, about fifty yards away.

He grabbed his Winchester .44 rifle and ran outside. Taking careful aim, he fired at Slade, the rearmost rider in the group. The outlaw slumped in the saddle and fell to the ground. He was later found to be dead. Before Jim could fire again, the remaining riders had passed out of sight round a bend in the street.

Jim shouted to the townspeople, who were coming out into the street, to help with the fire. Then he went back into the stable. Quickly, the bodies of Miles and Denton were dragged out into the street and the horses, squealing and rearing in terror, were led outside.

The fire had quickly taken a firm hold and it was touch and go before it was finally brought under control with the help of the townspeople.

Later in the day, Jim decided not to try and follow Vickery and his men, but to return to the Diamond R. He did not think that Vickery could have recognized him in the stable and he feared that the outlaw, when he found out that his brother had been captured with Jim's help, would assume that Jim had gone back to the Diamond R, and would himself head for the ranch to seek revenge. Jim wanted to be sure he was there when Vickery arrived.

Before he left Dodge he sent a telegraph message to a certain Morgan Jenkins in Amarillo.

SEVEN

Vickery had not recognized Jim as being one of the men in the stable, and as he rode out of Dodge, cursing the lawmen and nursing his injured hand, he wondered who could have betrayed them to the law. He decided to head for Indian Territory and his brother Brett's ranch, watching for any signs of pursuit on the way.

Half-way to the border with Indian Territory, Vickery rode into a small town, leaving the others waiting for him a mile outside town. He made his way to the doctor's house and had the wound on his hand treated and bandaged.

Seeing the grim look on Vickery's face, and sensing the rage boiling up inside him, the doctor decided not to ask how the wound had occurred. But he told the outlaw that the hand would never be the same again, and he'd better get himself a left-hand holster. Seething, Vickery left, and walked over to the store to buy some provisions for the journey.

Two days later they arrived at Brett Vickery's ranch in Indian Territory, only to find it deserted, with no sign of the horse herd that had been there on Josh Vickery's last visit. They rode on to Crispen, to see if they could pick up any news there of Brett Vickery and his men.

It wasn't long before they heard the story of Jim and Dillon bringing their three prisoners into town on a buckboard, and of Dillon and two other deputy US marshals leaving with the jail wagon taking the prisoners away for trial.

'Cochrane ain't going to get away with this,' said Vickery, his voice quivering with rage. 'I reckon he's back at the Diamond R by now. That's where we're going. When we get there, the first job is to take care of Cochrane. Then we'll get that rancher to hand some money over, so's to make the journey worth our while.

'On the way I'm going to pick up Bart Deakin. I heard he was staying in his hideout for a spell after that shooting in Wichita, when he killed the town marshal. I happen to know where that hide-out is.'

'Why do we need Deakin?' asked Gardner, curiously.

'I reckon we could do with his help on this job,' said Vickery. 'For one thing, I've got a feeling Cochrane's mighty handy with a gun, probably faster than you three. But I don't reckon he's a match for Deakin. I figure I used to be just about Deakin's equal myself, but that bullet I got in the hand in Dodge sure put paid to that. I want to make absolutely sure that Cochrane's finished for good this time.'

Before leaving Crispen, Vickery had his wounded hand attended to again by a doctor in town, who said it was healing satisfactorily.

Then they headed west through Indian Territory.

Early the following morning they reached the small ravine where Vickery expected to find Deakin. They rode slowly into the ravine, with hands raised, Vickery well ahead of the others.

They stopped when a man holding a rifle stepped out from behind a boulder and stood in front of Vickery.

'Howdy, Bart,' said Vickery.

'Josh,' said Deakin. He was a tall man, slightly stooped, with a pale face and a beaked nose. With a cold eye he inspected Vickery's companions, one by one, then gave his attention to Vickery.

'I need your help, Bart,' said the gang-leader as he dismounted. 'Can we talk about it?'

Deakin grunted and led the way to a small shack built against the side of the ravine. Vickery told his men to dismount and stay where they were, then followed Deakin into the shack.

He told the gunfighter of his encounters with Jim and of his wish that Deakin would take on the job of finishing him off for good.

'I don't know,' said Deakin. 'How much does the job pay?'

Vickery told him of his plan to get money from Ranger.

'I'll come along,' said Deakin, 'if I get the same share of the money as you take yourself.'

Vickery hesitated for a moment, then agreed. 'You ready to leave with us now?' he asked.

'I'll be ready in one hour,' replied Deakin.

At around the time that Deakin left his hideout with Vickery and his men, Jim rode up to the Diamond R ranch house. As he passed the barn two men holding rifles walked out and confronted him. Then one of them recognized him and waved him on. He dismounted outside the house and knocked on the door. It was opened by Miriam, who breathed a sigh of relief and smiled when she saw the man standing outside. Jim smiled back at her.

'You're all safe?' he asked.

'We're all safe,' she replied, 'and we've had some good news. Father's been getting some feeling in his legs lately and the doctor thinks that maybe he'll be able to walk normally before long.'

'That's great news,' said Jim.

'Come on in,' she said, and took him through to the living-room, where Ranger and his wife and son were seated at a table, just finishing a meal. At Emily Ranger's insistence, Jim sat down at the table and Miriam brought him some food.

When he had eaten, Jim told them about his recent encounters with Josh Vickery and his brother Brett.

'As you know,' he said, 'I had to kill Josh's nephew Earl and another of his men when I was bringing Joey back; and I was responsible, with Deputy Marshal Dillon, for the capture of his brother Brett.

'On account of all that,' he went on, 'I reckon it's pretty certain that Vickery'll come here with the idea of killing me. And when he's attended to that he wants to get his hands on as much of your money as he can. I don't think it'll be long before he and his gang turn up somewhere around here.'

'How do we stop them?' asked Ranger.

'We've got to be ready for them,' said Jim. 'How many ranch hands have you got now?'

'I signed two more on since you left,' said Ranger. 'I've got four hands now, not counting the cook. But they're cowhands, not fighting men.'

'I know,' said Jim. 'We'll just have to do the best we can. During daylight we need a look-out here to watch for riders coming from any direction. I figure you're doing that already?'

'We are,' confirmed the rancher.

'And during the night,' said Jim, 'I reckon we should have two night guards out to give the alarm if Vickery and his men show up. The four hands, with me and the cook, can cover that in shifts.'

'How many men d'you reckon Vickery'll have with him?' asked Ranger.

'Three,' replied Jim, 'maybe four, if he's

managed to replace the man he lost in Dodge. But I'm hoping to get some help. Before I left Dodge I telegraphed a man called Morgan Jenkins in Amarillo. I'm hoping he'll be here soon.

'He was a deputy of mine when I was a sheriff in Colorado. He was a first-rate lawman and a good friend of mine. He quit about six months before I did because his parents were in some sort of trouble in Amarillo. But I heard it's all cleared up now and I'm hoping he'll be able to lend us a hand. I can't think of anybody I'd sooner have on our side.

'You can't mistake him when he turns up. He's a mountain of a man, well over six feet and very strong. At the same time he's light on his feet and anything but clumsy in the way he handles a six-gun. He's got a deep bass voice and a laugh that can be heard half a mile away. He's about five years older than me.'

'When he turns up,' said Emily Ranger, 'he can share that room upstairs with you. We'll put another bunk in there.'

All was quiet on the ranch during the rest of that day and during the following day until noon, when Jim and the Rangers were taking a meal in the ranch house. A hand came to tell them that a lone rider was coming in from the south. Jim and the rancher went outside to await his arrival. Jim thought he recognized him. A minute later he was sure.

'It's Morgan,' he told Ranger. 'I'm feeling

happier already about our chances of getting the better of Vickery.'

Smiling, Morgan Jenkins rode up to them and dismounted from the big bay gelding he was riding. Jim shook hands and introduced him to the rancher.

'Got here as fast as I could when I got your message, Jim,' he said, in that deep voice of his. 'Couldn't imagine what trouble you've gotten yourself into now. I'm sure itching to find out what all this fuss is about.'

'Let's go inside,' said Ranger, and they all went through into the living-room, where the rancher introduced Morgan to his family. Jim explained to his friend why his help was so badly needed.

'That's quite a story,' said Morgan, when Jim had finished. 'You're pretty certain that Vickery's on his way?'

'I'm certain of it,' replied Jim.

Two days passed without any sign that Vickery and his men were in the area. Since Ranger had some business in the town and supplies were required from the store, it was decided that Ranger and Miriam would go on the buckboard into town, with Jim accompanying them on horse-back. Morgan would stay at the ranch house in case of trouble there.

They left around noon, after Jim had helped Ranger on to the buckboard and had lifted the wheelchair up behind him. When they reached Linford, Ranger stopped the buckboard outside the livery stable. The owner, Dan Gould, who was a friend of the rancher, came out to greet him and the others.

'Dan,' asked Ranger, 'have any strangers turned up in town the last day or two?'

'Only one, as far as I know,' replied the livery-man. 'He rode in this morning. Left his horse here and went over to the hotel on the other side of the street there. I don't know his name, or how long he's staying in town. He weren't exactly talkative.'

'What did he look like?' asked Jim.

'He was a hard man to figure,' replied Gould, 'but I'd put him down as a gunfighter, and a very dangerous man for anybody to tangle with. He's a tall thin man, clean-shaven, with a white face and a hooked nose, and a mean look in his eye. He's wearing black clothes, including a black Montana Peak hat. You'll sure know him if you see him.'

'I've read that description on Wanted notices a few times,' said Jim. 'I'm pretty sure he's a gunfighter called Deakin. He's wanted by the law for several murders. Is he still in the hotel?'

'Can't say for sure,' replied Gould. 'I've been working inside the stable. Maybe he's having a meal in there. His horse is still here, so he's in town somewhere.'

Deakin, seated in the hotel dining-room close to a window with a view out on to the street, saw Jim and the Rangers stop outside the livery stable. He had a description of Jim from Vickery which seemed to tally with the appearance of the man on horseback outside the stable.

He called over to a woman who was serving at the tables, and asked her if she knew the horseman and the people on the buckboard outside the stable.

'That's Mr Ranger of the Diamond R,' she told him, 'and his daughter Miriam. I think the man on the horse is helping out at the ranch. I don't know his name.'

Deakin grunted and the woman left. He pulled out his gun, a Colt .45, and checked that five chambers were loaded and that the gun moved smoothly in the holster. Then he paid for the meal and walked out of the hotel. He stopped on the boardwalk outside and looked towards the stable, where the rancher was finishing his conversation with Gould.

Glancing along the street, Gould saw Deakin. 'That's the stranger standing outside the hotel,' he said. The others turned round to look at the gunfighter, who was watching them intently. Studying him, Jim felt instinctively that the man spelt big trouble. He dismounted and spoke to Ranger.

'I have a feeling,' he said, 'that Deakin over there is a messenger from Vickery. Looks like he's hired a professional gunslinger to fight his battle for him. You two stay right here while I check him out.'

He walked along the street for twelve yards, to put the Rangers and Gould out of the line of fire.

Then he turned to face Deakin, who stepped down
from the boardwalk and slowly approached him.
Miriam's face whitened and the two men with her
tensed as Deakin drew closer to the man he
meant to kill. He stopped when Jim was still four
yards away.

'You Cochrane?' he asked, abruptly.

Jim nodded.

'I've got a bullet in my .45 for you,' said Deakin.
'It's a present from Josh Vickery. He asked me to
plug you some place where it hurt most and he
said he didn't want you to die too quick. I aim to
oblige him as soon as you're ready.'

He sneered as he watched Jim's face, watching
for the signs of fear and panic which his victims
usually displayed. But Jim looked anything but
scared. He stood nicely balanced, feet slightly
apart, calmly observing Deakin. His hand was
close to the handle of his Peacemaker.

'So Vickery was too scared to do the job himself,'
Jim observed. 'He had to bring in a two-bit
gunfighter like yourself, Deakin, to do his dirty
work. I've heard things about you. They say that
you really enjoy killing a man, especially when
the pay is good. But maybe your killing days are
over.'

Deakin flushed, and his hand brushed the
handle of his six-gun. He eyed Jim a little uncertainly. His victims were usually much more
subdued than the man in front of him.

'I'm waiting, Deakin,' said Jim. 'You beginning

to wonder whether you're fast enough to take me?'

Stung by Jim's remarks, Deakin went for his gun, but the usual swift smooth execution of his draw was affected by his anger, and his gun was cocked just a fraction of a second later than he would have wished.

Jim knew that a supreme effort was required from him if he was to stay alive. He forced himself to stay calm. He watched Deakin intently and started his draw at exactly the same time as his opponent. A moment later he knew that the speed of his own draw was surpassing anything that he had achieved before.

He fired at Deakin's chest, his bullet hitting its target just as Deakin pulled his own trigger. The gunfighter's body jerked as Jim's bullet hit him and Jim winced as the bullet from Deakin's six-gun nicked his right ear.

Momentarily, a look of shocked disbelief showed on Deakin's face as he stared at Jim. Then his legs buckled, and dropping his gun, he slumped to the ground, kicked once, and lay still. Jim walked up and bent down over him. A glance showed him that the gunfighter was dead, from a bullet in the heart.

Jim straightened up, looked at the small crowd of onlookers who had collected, then walked back to the buckboard.

The Rangers had watched the gun duel with considerable apprehension, and their relief was evident as Jim walked up them.

'It was Deakin all right,' he told them. 'He was sent by Vickery to finish me off. He's dead.'

He turned to Gould. 'Is there somebody around who can see that this man is buried?' he asked.

'I can fix that,' said Gould. 'There's a man in town who'll tend to it. And I'll get a message to the law in Amarillo telling them that Deakin's dead.'

'D'you happen to know,' asked Jim, 'which direction Deakin was coming from when he rode into town?'

'I didn't see him myself,' said Gould, 'but I happened to be chatting to a homesteader who drove his buckboard in soon after Deakin showed up. He told me he'd seen him riding in on an old trail that leaves town in an easterly direction and passes between two hills about three miles from here.'

'And you're sure he came in alone?' asked Jim.

'Not absolutely,' said Gould. 'Just wait here a minute.'

He walked along the street to an old-timer sitting on the porch of his shack. The two men conversed for a while, then Gould returned to the stable.

'Old Hank keeps a close watch on what goes on around here,' he said, 'and he's sure that Deakin came in alone, and that he's the only stranger that's been around here for the last week or so.'

Still a little shaken, Miriam walked along to the store, while Ranger drove on to the bank, accompanied by Jim, who helped him climb down from the buckboard and get in the wheelchair. Ranger went into the bank and when he came out half an hour later, he left the wheelchair and climbed on to the buckboard with Jim's help, then drove along to the store.

Jim helped the storekeeper load the provisions on the buckboard, then Miriam climbed aboard and they set off for the Diamond R. Jim rode alongside the rancher.

'You had us both worried back there,' said Ranger. 'That sure was a mean-looking man.'

'I was lucky,' said Jim. 'His bullet nicked my ear. We can be fairly sure now that Vickery and his men are hiding out somewhere around here, and Vickery ain't likely to give up just because Deakin's cashed in. But what his next move will be is hard to guess.

'Now that Morgan's here I have a mind to try and find out where Vickery and his men are hiding out, so that we can carry the fight to them. While I'm looking around, Morgan could stay with you on the ranch, in case any of them show up there.'

'That sounds like a dangerous thing you're aiming to do,' said Miriam. 'Why don't we all stay together?'

'Because that's probably what he's expecting us to do,' Jim replied. 'I reckon we should try and find out where they are, and how many men Vickery has with him. That's something we need to know. And one man on his own stands less chance of being spotted by them. My guess is that they're hanging around somewhere not too far away from here, waiting for Deakin to ride back and tell them I'm dead.'

'Those two hills Gould mentioned,' said Ranger, pointing towards the east. 'You can see them over there. The trail goes right between them.'

'I reckon it's possible,' said Jim, 'that the gang's hiding somewhere over in that direction. I aim to ride out there after dark and see if I can find them.'

When they reached the ranch house Jim told Morgan about the gunfight in Linford and about his intention to ride out after dark to try and locate the gang.

'I'll go with you,' said Morgan.

'No,' said Jim, 'I'll be a lot happier with you here, in case Vickery decides to strike during the night. If I do find out where the gang's hiding out, you can be sure I ain't going to risk being taken. I'll come back here and we'll decide what to do next.'

EIGHT

Jim set out just after nightfall, heading straight for the two hills between which Deakin had ridden on his way into town. He had the advantage of the dim light from a half moon which was riding in the sky, and he made steady progress.

Passing between the two hills he rode on in the same direction for a further six miles, when he reached a flat-topped ridge running across his path. This ridge formed the boundary of the Diamond R range. He dismounted at the foot of the ridge and led his horse up the steep slope towards the top.

Reaching the top he looked along the ridge, then down both sides, hoping that he might see a glimmer of light from a camp-fire. But none was visible. He rode north along the flat top of the ridge, which rose slowly towards a small peak he could see outlined against the night sky about half a mile away. As he rode along, he continued to look down both sides of the ridge.

Reaching the foot of the peak, which, so far as he could judge, reared some two hundred feet skyward, he dismounted, and securing his horse at the base, he carefully climbed the steep rocky slope. Soon, breathing heavily, he was standing on the top, which was in the form of a rough circle of almost flat ground about forty feet in diameter.

He slowly circled this area, surveying the ground below, looking for the tell-tale pinpoint of light which might indicate a camp-fire. But he was disappointed. Three slow circuits of the top revealed nothing. He sat down and rested for a while, then made one more circuit, with the same result. He decided to return to his horse.

He started to turn, in order to walk towards the point at which he had reached the top, when the corner of his eye registered the faintest glimmer of light from a point to the north-east, some distance away. He turned his head and looked directly towards it. The light flared up a little as he watched, then died down until it was barely visible.

Using the North Star, which was bright in the northern sky, Jim was able to fix the direction of the light from his present position. He climbed down to his horse, led it slowly down the slope of the ridge, and headed towards what he hoped was Vickery's camp.

He had noticed for a while that the sky was darkening, and he put on his slicker and continued at walking pace as a torrential rainstorm

passed over the area. It was more than half an
hour before it ceased and the sky cleared. He
stopped and looked ahead. There was no sign of
the light he had seen from the peak.

He carried on until he judged that he was somewhere near the source of the light he had seen
earlier, but he could still see no sign of it. He
carried on, and found himself riding along the top
of an almost sheer slope leading down into a
narrow ravine.

Looking down into it he could see, about three
hundred yards down the ravine, the glow of a
camp-fire, with some men sitting close to it. He
tethered his horse to a small bush well back from
the ravine, then, taking advantage of all available
cover, he made a careful search for look-outs. He
found only one guard, Rothery, stationed at the
mouth of the ravine, where it gave way to a
stretch of flat ground. He retraced his steps, for
about two hundred yards, to a point at the top of
the wall of the ravine which was level with the
camp-fire. He lay down in a position from which
he could look over the edge and down a steep
slope to the floor of the ravine. He could feel the
wetness of the sodden ground through his clothing.

There were four men seated around the camp-
fire, which was now burning well on the floor of
the ravine. Immediately, Jim recognized Vickery,
who was sitting facing him. Then he saw Bellamy
and Gardner. The fourth man, a stranger to him,

was a half-breed called Parker whom Vickery had picked up on his way through Indian Territory.

Jim watched the men down below for a while. They were obviously chatting to one another, but they were too far away for him to make out what they were saying. He decided to go back to the ranch with the information he had managed to obtain so far.

But as he was rising to his feet, the sodden ground underneath him suddenly gave way and amid a shower of earth and small rocks he found himself sliding uncontrollably down the steep slope. As he reached the bottom his body slewed round and he started to reach for his Peacemaker. But before he could draw it his head struck a rock projecting from the ground and he fell, unconscious, among the debris which had fallen from above.

At the sound of the landslide, Vickery and the others jumped up and ran over to the debris lying on the ground. Seeing the figure sprawled among it, they dragged it out and over to the fire. Vickery turned the body over so that the face was illuminated by the flames.

'Cochrane!' he shouted. 'This *is* a stroke of luck. It looks like we didn't need Deakin after all.'

He bent down over Jim and saw the large bruise on his forehead. He took out the Peacemaker, which was still in Jim's holster.

'He's knocked out,' he said. 'Should be coming round soon. I'm wondering what's happened to Deakin.'

Jim came round a few minutes later. Shakily, he sat up, shook his head and scanned the four faces in front of him. He felt for his gun, but the holster was empty. He looked at Vickery, who was regarding him with a look of hostility which boded ill for the prisoner.

'I'm surprised to see you here, Cochrane,' he said. 'I sent a friend of mine called Deakin to take care of you. It's clear he hasn't had a chance to meet up with you yet.'

'We met up all right,' said Jim, 'but Deakin wasn't quite fast enough. Come daylight, he's due to be planted in the graveyard in Linford.'

Vickery's face purpled and he had difficulty controlling his rage. When he spoke, the menace in his voice was unmistakable.

'I still don't know, Cochrane, how you managed to get away from my brother. But you ain't going to get away from me.'

He told Bellamy and Gardner to bind Jim hand and foot and lay him near the fire. Then he spoke to his men.

'I have the same idea as my brother Brett had,' he said. 'After what he done to us both, I want this man to die slow, wishing all the time that we'd shot him through the head in the first place. I'd like some ideas about how we could fix this. How about you, Parker?'

'I was living with some Apache Indians in Arizona for a while,' said the half-breed. 'They hunted down a white man who had killed their chief. They took him back to their village and trussed him up so tight that he couldn't move his arms or legs. Then they dug a hole in the ground and stood him up in it so that when the hole was filled in, only his head was sticking out.

'The loose earth around him was rammed down real tight,' Parker went on, 'and the only move-ment the man could make was a turn of the head. He was just left like that, out in the hot sun, with no food and drink.'

'That sounds just about right,' said Vickery. 'How long did he last?'

'I don't know,' replied Parker. 'I left seven days after he'd been captured and he was still alive then. But I could see from the look on his face that he was really suffering. Apart from sunburn and hunger and thirst, I guess the way he was held tight in the ground like that, not being able to move anything below the neck, was pretty hard to bear.'

'That settles it,' said Vickery. 'Come daylight, we'll find a piece of soft ground out in the open and dig a hole for Cochrane. Meanwhile, leave him where he is, and we'll take turns watching him through the night. And one of you'd better go find his horse and bring it here.'

It was a long night for Jim, under surveillance all the time, and suffering the discomfort of being tightly bound – hand and foot. After breakfast, which was denied Jim, Vickery selected a place close by, in the middle of the ravine, where there was a patch of soft ground.

Using a large knife to loosen the earth and a pan to scoop up the loose soil and throw it aside, Parker and Rothery laboriously dug out a hole wide and deep enough to take Jim's body. Meantime, Gardner, under Vickery's direction, trussed the prisoner so thoroughly that, apart from wiggling his fingers and toes, he was incapable of movement below the neck.

Jim was lifted up by two of the men and placed, feet first, into the hole, with his head facing south. Then the hole was filled in, the loose material being rammed down hard with the trunk cut from a small nearby tree.

When the job was finished, the outlaws stood in a semi-circle looking down at Jim's head. There was a look of grim satisfaction on Vickery's face.

'This is the end of the road for you, Cochrane,' he said. 'We'll leave you buried here for a while, then, if we have to leave in a hurry, and you're still alive, we'll shoot you through the head.'

Jim stared back at the outlaw. Already he was feeling discomfort due to his inability to move his limbs, but he showed no sign of this on his face.

'I'm curious,' he said. 'Now that you ain't got me to bother about, what d'you aim to do with the Rangers?'

'We're going to squeeze as much money out of them as we can,' replied Vickery. 'I happen to know that Ranger's a rich man. Maybe it'll take him a few days to get his hands on the money, but we'll hold his wife, and that son and daughter of his on the ranch till he comes up with it. Then we'll come back here and tend to you if you're still alive. A bullet through the head should do the trick.'

Jim made no reply, and Vickery turned to Bellamy.

'We're leaving for the Diamond R well before nightfall,' he said. 'I want you to stay here with Cochrane. Don't feed him or give him water. Just watch him to make sure nobody comes along and tries to dig him out of that hole.'

Vickery and three of his men left in the afternoon. As they rode out of the ravine, a veteran prospector, Henry Rafferty, who had led his mule and burro into a small grove of trees nearby to take a temporary respite, spotted the group of riders. He led the two animals further into the grove and watched unnoticed as the riders passed by and rode off to the east. He didn't like the look of them and was relieved that he hadn't met them in the open.

He looked over towards the ravine, about a quarter of a mile away from which the men had emerged. Inside it, not far from the entrance, smoke was rising. He studied it for a while and decided it was probably from a camp-fire.

Reason told him to give the ravine a miss and ride out of the area as fast as he could. But curiosity won the day, even though it had got him into numerous scrapes in the past. He tethered the mule and the burro, took a pair of battered field-glasses from one of the packs, and checked that there was no one in sight in the vicinity of the ravine.

He left the grove and headed for the wall of the ravine, taking advantage of any cover available. When he reached it, he bent down and moved along it, out of sight of anyone down below, until he was level with the rising smoke. He lay down and crawled through a patch of brush until he could look down into the ravine.

There appeared to be only one man down below. He was squatting by the fire, drinking something from a large mug. As Rafferty looked up and down the ravine, his eye was caught by a curious round object on the ground, not far from the fire.

He studied it through the field-glasses and suddenly realized, when it moved slightly, that he was looking at a human head. As he watched, the man who had been squatting by the fire walked up to the buried man with a mug of water, waved it tantalizingly in his face, then poured it on to the ground in front of his eyes. Then, laughing uproariously, he walked back to the fire, which was burning brightly, and squatted down again.

Rafferty decided to get a closer look at the prisoner. He crept back along the top of the wall of the ravine until he was directly above the buried man and looking down towards his face. He focused his field-glasses on the prisoner's head.

With a start, he realized he was looking at an old acquaintance of his, Jim Cochrane, one time sheriff in East Colorado. Jim, out riding one day, on the way to investigate some robberies at a miners' camp, had come across Rafferty lying on the ground and bleeding badly, with a bullet inside him. The prospector had been robbed of his bag of gold dust, all he had to show for many years of prospecting, and had been left for dead. Jim had got him to a doctor just in time, and had later tracked the robbers down and got the old man's gold dust back.

Rafferty decided that he had to help Jim, but thought that he had better wait till well after nightfall, when there would be a better chance of his being able to deal with the man who was guarding Jim.

The light was fading as he went back to his mule and pulled from a saddle holster his old American Arms 12-gauge shotgun. He loaded it, had something to eat and drink, then, carrying the shotgun, he returned to his previous position at the top of the ravine wall.

By the light of the moon and the camp-fire, which Bellamy kept well alight, Rafferty watched Jim and the guard. Just before eleven o'clock Bellamy threw some more wood on the fire, then put down his bedroll and lay on it, pulling a blanket over his body. He turned over a couple of times, then fell still.

Carrying his shotgun, Rafferty moved back to the mouth of the canyon, entered it, and crouching down, he moved slowly towards the sleeping

guard. Jim heard him coming and, not recogniz-
ing him in the dim light, he watched Rafferty as
he passed, a few yards away, his eyes fixed on
Bellamy.

At the time, Jim was suffering from an excruciating cramp in his left leg and a severe itch in his
right leg which he was unable to scratch. He
turned his head to keep Rafferty in view.

Treading as softly as he could, the prospector
was within twelve feet of the outlaw when his foot
struck a small stone which rolled away from him
towards the sleeping man. The slight sound
disturbed Bellamy, who sat up, desperately grab-
bing a six-shooter lying by his side, with the
intention of firing at the intruder.

But Rafferty's shotgun was already pointed at
Bellamy and he pulled the trigger before the
outlaw was ready to fire. The wide blast pattern of
the shotgun gave Bellamy no chance. The lethal
charge of buckshot slammed him to the ground,
dying as he fell.

Rafferty walked up and bent down over the
outlaw. He could see that he posed no further
threat. He walked back to Jim and knelt down
against him, looking into his face. Jim stared at
him in astonishment.

'Henry Rafferty?' he queried, hoarsely.

'The same,' replied Rafferty. 'Just repaying an
old debt. That man over there ain't going to give
us any trouble. First thing to do is get you out of
there. I've got a pick and shovel on my burro. I'll

go for them. Be back in a few minutes.'

When Rafferty returned he set about freeing Jim. As he worked in the moonlight, Jim told him how he came to be in such a predicament, and Rafferty explained his own presence there. It took the old man over an hour before he had dug down to Jim's feet.

Breathing heavily, he pulled a knife from his belt and felt for the ropes around Jim's body. He cut through them to free the limbs. The pain was excruciating as Jim gradually flexed his arms and legs while his circulation returned to normal. It was quite some time before, with Rafferty's help, he was able to clamber out of the hole and stand unsteadily on the ground above.

'I sure am obliged to you, Henry,' he said. 'I figured I was done for. What I'm going to do now is head for the Diamond R and see what Vickery's up to. Maybe I can put a spoke in his wheel.'

'You need any help?' asked Rafferty.

'Thanks, Henry,' Jim replied, 'but you've done enough already. What I'm going to do now, I can do better on my own. But I'd better have some food and drink first.'

When he had satisfied his hunger and thirst, Jim picked up Bellamy's revolver, brushed himself well down, and went for his horse, which was tethered further up the ravine. He thanked Rafferty again, and the old man told him he was heading north-east for Denver, and intended to travel a few miles before making camp.

They parted outside the ravine, and Jim headed for the ranch. He had ridden about nine miles when he thought he heard the sound of approaching riders ahead on his right.

He rode his horse into a small hollow on his left, dismounted, and ran to lie down and look over the rim of the hollow. He saw the dim shapes of two horses and riders a hundred yards away, moving fast in the direction from which he had just come. He wondered who the riders were. When they had disappeared from view Jim mounted, and continued his ride towards the Diamond R.

NINE

When Vickery and his men left Jim buried up to his neck in the ravine, guarded by Bellamy, they rode towards the Diamond R, reaching the vicinity of the ranch buildings around half past eleven in the evening. They stopped at a point where the darkness put them just out of sight of anyone in or around the buildings. Lights were visible in the house and the bunkhouse. As they watched, the lights in the bunkhouse went out, then the lights in the house.

They waited a little longer, then Vickery spoke to Parker, the half-breed. Parker, who was half Apache, had an uncanny ability, which he had demonstrated to Vickery on a number of occasions in the past, for stalking an enemy in the dark.

'I reckon they'll have guards out,' said Vickery. 'Go in there, find out where they are, and see if you can take care of them without waking the others.'

Parker nodded, and checked the knife on his

belt. Then he melted into the darkness. Within twenty minutes he had established that two of Ranger's hands had been posted as guards, one outside the house and one near the bunkhouse.

He despatched the one near the bunkhouse first, creeping up noiselessly behind the man and stabbing him in the back. Then he moved up on the one outside the house, and dealt with him in the same way, before returning to Vickery and the others to report that the way was now clear for a surprise attack.

They rode up to the corral fence and tied their horses to it. Vickery sent Gardner and Parker to the bunkouse, to go inside and tie the ranch hands up and gag them, at gunpoint. When this had been done, Parker stayed in the bunkhouse, on guard, and Gardner rejoined Vickery and Rothery. The three outlaws made for the ranch house.

Finding the door open, they crept inside, and Vickery lit an oil lamp standing on a table. Carrying the lamp, he headed for the room which he knew, from his previous visit, to be the bedroom of Ranger and his wife. He told Rothery to stand guard outside the bedroom door. Then he opened the door, and walked inside, followed by Gardner, who closed the door behind him.

The rancher and his wife woke simultaneously and sat up in bed. Apprehensive, they stared at Vickery as he walked over to them, a six-gun in one hand, the lamp in the other. He placed the lamp on a bedside table and lit a second one already there.

'Where are the boy and girl?' he asked.

'Both upstairs in bed,' replied Ranger. 'What d'you want with us?'

'I've got some news for you, Ranger,' said Vickery. 'Your friend Cochrane came looking for us and got himself killed. So we've come here looking for money. Until we get it, we're holding you and your family prisoner. First thing tomorrow you'll go into town to make arrangements to get hold of what we're after. Thirty thousand dollars is what we want. We know you're worth that – and a lot more.'

'Twenty thousand dollars is the most I can get hold of quickly,' said the rancher, truthfully.

'I'm sure you can do better than that,' said Vickery, walking round to Emily's side of the bed. He twisted her arm and pulled it up behind her back until she cried out in agony. Ranger, incensed, pulled out the gun concealed under his pillow and swung it round towards Vickery. But before it had moved round sufficiently to bear on its target, Gardner fired at the rancher's chest, from only a few feet away. The rancher fell backwards, with a bullet in his heart. His wife screamed. Vickery silenced her with a blow to the face. Then he moved round the bed to have a look at Ranger. He bent down over him, then turned to Gardner.

'You fool!' he said. 'You've just lost us thirty

thousand dollars. We ain't got a chance of getting our hands on the money with Ranger dead. All we can do now is to see if we can find any money in the house before we leave.'

Fuming, he picked up Ranger's revolver and walked to the door. He opened it and spoke to Rothery.

'Stand near the bottom of the stairs,' he said, 'and watch for the boy and girl coming down. Chase them back if they do.'

He looked at Emily Ranger, cradling her dead husband in her arms. He told Gardner to pick up one of the lighted lamps, then they both left the room, locking the door behind them. They walked over to a safe at the far end of the living-room and Gardner placed the lamp on top of it. The safe was standing beside a large desk which was close to the door leading to the outside of the house.

Morgan, in his room upstairs, woke to the sound of a gunshot somewhere nearby, whether inside or outside the house, he could not tell. He was lying on the bed, fully dressed, ready to take his turn at guard duty.

He jumped out of bed, put his gunbelt on, silently opened the door of his room and stepped into the passage outside. At the same time he heard Miriam come out of the room next door.

'Go into Joey's room,' he whispered to her, 'and stay in there. I'll go and see who fired that shot.'

She turned, walked along the passage to the door of Joey's room, and went inside. Morgan drew his gun and softly descended the stairs to the sharp bend half-way down. He stopped as he heard movements down below and saw the dim light from a lamp in the living-room shining on the wall of the staircase. He risked a quick look round the bend in the staircase and saw a man, a stranger to him, standing at the bottom, with a gun in his hand, looking towards the end of the living-room.

Treading softly, gun in hand, Morgan quickly moved round the bend in the staircase to confront the man standing at the bottom. A squeaking stair-tread alerted Rothery, who turned to face Morgan, raising his gun. Before he could fire, Morgan shot him through the head and he fell.

Morgan ran down the stairs and across the room, heading for the rear of a large armchair. As he crossed the room he looked to his left, towards the lamp, and took a snap shot at Gardner, who was standing by the safe. Gardner had his gun cocked, ready to shoot, but his shot went wide. Before he could fire again he was hit in the chest by the bullet from Morgan's six-gun. He fell, and lay motionless.

When Rothery was shot, Vickery was behind the safe, examining the back of it. He sank down behind it at the sound of the shot, then heard two more shots and saw Gardner fall down by the side of the safe. He stayed where he was, listening for sounds of movement in the room.

Morgan, looking from behind the armchair,

could see that neither of the two men he had shot down was moving, and that there appeared to be no one else in the room. He waited a couple of minutes, then, seeing that the two were still motionless, he moved from behind the chair, gun in hand, and walked over to Rothery.

As he bent down to look at the outlaw, he saw, out of the corner of his eye, a movement near the safe. Turning quickly, he saw Vickery standing behind it, a six-gun in his hand. He dodged to one side, but was too late. The bullet hit him in the left side of his chest as he fired at Vickery. He staggered, then ran back to the shelter of the armchair. Vickery, hit in the left shoulder, sank down behind the safe.

From behind the chair, despite his wound, Morgan fired two more shots towards Vickery, then lost consciousness and collapsed on the floor behind the chair. Vickery, wondering who it could be who had wounded him and disposed of two of his men, slid the lamp off the top of the safe and blew it out. Then, in the darkness, and screened by the desk and safe, he crawled on hands and knees to the door leading outside, and opened it just wide enough for him to pass through.

Once outside, he decided there was no point now, with himself wounded and two of his men dead, in hanging around the Diamond R. Holding his wounded shoulder, he ran to the bunkhouse and called Parker out. Then they both ran to their horses and rode off.

When Morgan came to, he pulled himself to his feet. Through the open door he could see the night sky. Slowly, he walked over to the door and listened for sounds outside. He heard the sound of riders, gradually fading away. He turned, lit a lamp standing on a table, then walked slowly to the Rangers' bedroom door, unlocked it, and went inside.

Emily Ranger was cradling her husband's head in her arms. She looked up, distraught, as Morgan entered. He walked over and looked down at Ranger. He could see that the rancher was dead.

'I'm sorry,' he said. 'Who did it?'

'It was one of Vickery's men,' she replied.

'The live ones have left,' said Morgan. 'I'll call Miriam.'

He walked to the foot of the stairs and called Miriam. She came down with Joey. They saw the two bodies on the floor.

'Your father has been killed, Miriam,' said Morgan. 'Will you help your mother? She needs you. I'm going outside, to see what's happened to the men.'

Shocked, Miriam walked into the bedroom and sat on the bed by the side of her mother. Joey followed her.

Morgan went outside and headed for the bunkhouse. As he walked, he weaved from side to side, and twice he had to pause until an attack of dizziness abated. On his way he passed the bodies of the two hands who had been knifed by Parker.

Inside the bunkhouse he found the two hands

struggling to free themselves. As he cut the ropes around them he told them that Ranger and two hands had been killed, also two of the outlaws. He said he was sure the remaining outlaws had left. Then he lost consciousness.

The two hands carried him back to the ranch house and laid him on a couch in the living-room. Then they dragged the bodies of the two outlaws out of the house. Coming out of the bedroom, Miriam saw Morgan and called her mother. Emily Ranger left the dead body of her husband to tend to Morgan's wound, which was bleeding profusely. With Miriam helping, she removed Morgan's vest and shirt and closely inspected the wound.

'Is it bad?' asked Miriam.

'It's not so good,' replied her mother. 'The bullet went right through his side, and it's done a lot of damage. That's why it's bleeding so fast. We've got to stop that, or he'll die.'

She went for a clean sheet, and tearing some strips off it, she made a thick pad to place over the wound, and bound it in position. As she was finishing, Morgan opened his eyes and looked at the bandage.

'Is there a bullet in there?' he asked.

'No,' she replied. 'You were lucky.'

She went over to comfort Miriam and Joey, who were standing nearby. Moments later they all looked towards the door as it opened and Jim walked in. Emily Ranger stared at him as if he were a ghost.

'Vickery told Will and me you were dead,' she said.

'I was good as dead,' said Jim, 'but I had a stroke of luck. I've just seen the bodies and the hands outside. The men told me what's happened here. Vickery told me that he and his men were coming here, but they were holding me prisoner at the time and there wasn't anything I could do about it. Two riders just passed me in the dark, about three miles north-east of here. I wasn't close enough to tell who they were, but I reckon they must have been Vickery and Parker.'

He walked over to Morgan. 'How're you feeling, Morgan?' he asked.

'A mite shaky,' said his friend, 'but I'll be all right.'

'He needs to see a doctor,' said Emily Ranger. 'The bullet went through, but it left a nasty mess behind.'

She called in one of the hands from outside and told him to ride to Linford and bring Doc Culver back with him, and while he was there, to ask the undertaker to come out to the ranch as quick as he could.

While they were waiting for the doctor, Morgan told Jim that, as well as killing two of the outlaws in the house, he was sure he had hit the third, who must have been Vickery. He had seen a small pool of blood on the floor near the door through which Vickery had left the house.

The hand, returning with the doctor three

hours later, said that the undertaker would set off from Linford at first light.

The doctor went into the bedroom to see Ranger. He came out after a short while and spoke to Emily Ranger and her son and daughter for a few minutes. Then he took Morgan's bandage off and closely examined the wound.

'You're a lucky man,' he said. 'A few inches to one side, and that bullet would have killed you. As it is, when I've cleaned the wound up and we've got the bleeding stopped, it should heal up pretty well, provided you stay in bed a week or so.'

They buried Will Ranger the following day, on a hillside not far from the ranch house. The two hands and the outlaws were buried in the town cemetery just outside Linford.

In the evening, Emily Ranger, Miriam and Jim met together in Morgan's bedroom to discuss the future.

'Have you decided whether you're going to stay on here, Mrs Ranger?' Jim asked.

'Of course,' she replied. 'Will and I worked hard to make this spread what it is, and I reckon to hand it over to Joey one day.'

'There's one thing *I* have to do,' said Jim, 'and that is to capture Vickery. First, he's a killer, who's got be stopped, and second, that twisted mind of his might send him back here for revenge, when he's built his gang up again. And we don't want to be sitting here, wondering all the time if and when he and his gang are going to turn up.'

'I'm going with you,' said Morgan, 'if you can wait till the doc says I'm fit to ride.'

'I can wait,' said Jim, 'and I'll sure be glad of your company.'

He turned to Emily Ranger. 'It looks like me and Morgan are going to be here for a week or so before we can start out after Vickery,' he said, 'but after that you'll need help here, and on top of that, I'm worried that Vickery might come back here before we can locate him. So what I'm going to do is telegraph my father and ask him if he'd send his foreman, Don Martin, down here with two hands to help you and your hands out till we get back.

'Don Martin is a good man,' he went on. 'He's an ex-Army officer, and pretty handy with a gun.'

'That would be a big help,' she said, 'but are you sure your father will be able to spare them for a while?'

'I'm sure,' replied Jim. 'I'm going to town first thing tomorrow to telegraph him. I had another idea as well,' he went on. 'I'd be a lot happier if you and Miriam and Joey lived in town till we get back. You can leave it to Don Martin to run the ranch for a spell. He's absolutely reliable.'

Emily Ranger thought for a moment before she replied, reluctantly.

'I guess you're right,' she said, 'when you say that Vickery might come back. A good friend of mine, Grace Carlton, runs a boarding-house in Linford. I'm sure she'll find room for us.'

The following morning Jim accompanied the Rangers to the boarding-house in town. Then he sent the telegraph message to his father, telling him of the killing of Ranger, explaining the present situation, and asking him for the temporary help of Martin and two hands.

Five days later, Martin rode in with two men, and Jim introduced them to Morgan, who was well on the way to recovery. He fully explained the situation, telling Martin that he and Morgan would be heading after Vickery as soon as Morgan was fit to ride.

'You can count on us to take care of things at this end,' said Martin.

'I know I can,' said Jim. 'I'm hoping to catch up with Vickery before he gets round to thinking of coming back here, but watch out for him, just in case.'

'I'll do that,' said Martin.

The following morning, Jim took Martin into town to meet the Ranger family.

TEN

A week later, Jim and Morgan were ready to leave on Vickery's trail. First, they rode into town to see the Rangers.

'We're all right here,' said Emily Ranger, 'but we'll be glad when we can all go back home.'

'I'll let you know how things are going,' said Jim. 'Meanwhile, stay in town. You can be sure that Don Martin's doing a good job out at the ranch. He'll come into town regular to report to you how things are going.'

Jim had a few minutes alone with Miriam before they left.

'This is another time that you're taking off,' she said, 'leaving me wondering if we'll ever see you again.'

'It's got to be done, Miriam,' he said.

'I know that,' she replied. 'But it don't make it any easier.'

'I've been thinking,' said Jim, 'that when I get back, we should look around for a preacher. It's time we got married. Then maybe I can pitch in and help your mother run the ranch for a spell if she'd like me to. How does the idea strike you?'

'You're a good man, Jim Cochrane,' she said, 'helping us out like you did. I'm all in favour of that idea of yours. I'll see how mother feels about it after you've left. I reckon she'll feel just the same way as I do. We'll all be praying for you both while you're away.'

Jim kissed her and walked over to Morgan who was already mounted and ready to leave. They headed straight for the ravine where Jim had recently been captured by Vickery, figuring that the outlaw would have headed there to attend to Jim's demise and pick up Bellamy.

When they arrived at the ravine they found evidence that Vickery and Parker had been there. Bellamy's body had been hurriedly covered with stones and two heavily-bloodstained bandages, which could have been used by Vickery, had been left on the ground.

Jim showed Morgan the pit in which he had been buried. Then they looked around for tracks leaving the ravine. There were faint indications that, a while ago, two riders had left the ravine, then headed east.

'I'm sure they're heading for Indian Territory,' said Jim. 'When I was a prisoner here, I heard Rothery and Gardner talking about a hideout Vickery often used there. It seems he shared it with another outlaw gang led by a man called Messiter. As to where it's located, the only information I picked up was that it's about twenty-six miles south of the Kansas border, which ain't a lot of use to us.

'But we know that Vickery's wounded, maybe badly. As far as I know, there's no doctor between here and the border, but once he's crossed over, it's likely he's going to look around for the nearest one. There ain't no point in us trying to follow old tracks from here. We'll head due east for the border and start nosing around as soon as we're in Indian Territory.'

Two days later they crossed the border early in the morning and continued east for about two hours, when they spotted a small isolated group of buildings ahead, to the right. They headed towards them, and as they drew nearer they could see one large building with the words ELI SMITH – GENERAL STORE painted roughly on the front wall, and a couple of large sheds with big double doors. The store looked somewhat out of place in an area which appeared to be completely devoid of other habitations. There were no horses at the hitching rail outside the store. They dismounted and went inside.

There was only one man in the store, stacking some goods on the shelves. A stout, bald, middle-aged man, wearing an apron, he turned to face them as they walked in. Then he moved behind the counter. Jim bought a few supplies, then he asked the storekeeper where the nearest doctor was located.

'I've got a bad pain in the belly,' he explained. 'Had it about a week. Just can't get rid of it.'

'Nearest one is Doc Sawyer, just over twenty miles south-east of here,' said Smith. 'He's in a small town called Calico. I reckon,' he went on, 'that Sawyer owes me some commission. You're the second patient I'll have sent him in the past two weeks.'

'What was wrong with the other one?' asked Jim, curiously.

'He didn't say,' replied Smith, 'and I didn't have the nerve to ask him. He was a hard-looking *hombre* with a scarred cheek. He didn't look too good, and the way he was holding himself, I got the idea that maybe he had a gunshot wound in the shoulder. He rode in with a half-breed around two weeks ago. They bought some bandages and a few other things, then they rode off.'

Outside the store, Jim and Morgan paused before mounting their horses.

'That was a stroke of luck, us calling in here,' said Jim. 'We'll head for Calico, and see if we can find out from that doctor how badly Vickery's injured and, if we're lucky, where he is now.'

They rode into Calico, twenty miles south of the Kansas border, in mid-afternoon. Moving along the dusty deserted street, they soon located the DOCTOR sign outside a neat, white-painted house right on the edge of town. They dismounted, and Jim knocked on the door.

It was opened by a good-looking woman in her

late twenties, who identified herself as the doctor's wife. Jim thought there was a worried look about her, and he wondered what was bothering her. He asked if they could see the doctor.

She led them into a room and left. Shortly after, the doctor came in. He was a neatly dressed man in his early thirties. Jim introduced himself and Morgan. He told Sawyer that they were both ex-lawmen, and were following the trail of an outlaw Josh Vickery and one of his men. They hoped to catch up with the two outlaws and hand them over to the law.

Jim went on to tell Sawyer that he thought that Vickery might have been to see him about two weeks ago to get some treatment for a gunshot wound. He described Vickery, and asked the doctor if this was the case, and whether he knew anything about the outlaws' present whereabouts.

As Jim finished speaking, Sawyer cleared his throat, then replied. He seemed a little nervous.

'Sorry, I can't help,' he said. 'I haven't seen the man you're talking about, and I haven't needed to treat a gunshot wound for quite a while. The man you're talking about must have gone somewhere else for help. I've got to leave you now. I have a patient to visit.' Hastily, he ushered Jim and Morgan out of the house and closed the door behind them.

'That was an interesting conversation,' said Jim. 'I've got a strong feeling that the doctor's lying. I wonder why?'

'I got the same feeling,' said Morgan. 'I think the two of them are running scared.'

'Let's ask a few questions around town,' suggested Jim. 'Maybe somebody saw Vickery and Parker here.'

But visits to the store, livery stable, hotel and saloon drew a blank. They went into a small dining-room inside the hotel for a meal.

'I had the feeling,' said Morgan, 'that the folks we've just been speaking to were all telling the truth when they said they hadn't seen Vickery and Parker. So where do we go from here?'

'I think you're right,' said Jim. 'We'll just . . .' He broke off as he saw the doctor's wife come into the dining-room, look around, and walk over towards them. She stopped at their table and spoke to Jim.

'Mr Cochrane,' she said. 'When you and your friend have finished your meal, would you please come over to our place? We have something to tell you.'

'The meal can wait,' said Jim. 'We'll come with you right now.'

They all sat down in the living-room in the doctor's house.

'Since you left,' said Dr Sawyer, 'my wife's convinced me that we should tell you the truth about the man you say is Vickery.'

He went on to tell them that Vickery and a half-breed had knocked him up at two in the morning about two weeks ago, to attend to a gunshot wound in Vickery's shoulder. Vickery was in bad shape, barely able to walk. He had a bullet inside him which Sawyer had some difficulty in prising out. When he had cleaned the wound and bandaged the shoulder, it was clear that the outlaw was not capable of riding a horse.

The half-breed had forced Sawyer, at gunpoint, to hitch up the buggy he used when visiting patients out of town. Then the half-breed had helped Vickery out and into the buggy, and Sawyer had been ordered to take the reins. By his side, Vickery held a six-gun in his hand. Sawyer was ordered to follow Parker, and his wife was told to say nothing about the outlaws' visit if she wanted to get her husband back unharmed.

'I followed him about seven miles to the south-east,' said Sawyer, 'before he led me into a ravine which was pretty obviously being used as an outlaws' hideout. A look-out challenged us at the entrance to the ravine, then roused the camp, and Vickery was carried into a cabin and laid on a bunk.

'I had another look at his wound,' Sawyer went on, 'then they said I could leave. But they told me to go back there in two days' time to check up on Vickery's condition. And they threatened that if I said anything to anybody about Vickery's visit to Calico and about his present whereabouts, they'd see that my wife suffered for it. They actually hinted that a few knife-cuts on her face wouldn't improve her appearance any.'

'You went out to see Vickery again?' asked Jim.

'Yes,' replied Sawyer, 'two days later. He was doing all right. I told him it would be safe for him to ride in a couple of weeks' time, and that there was no need for me to see him again.'

'How many men were there at the camp, as well as Vickery and the half-breed?' asked Jim.

'Five that I saw,' replied Sawyer. 'One of them was a Mexican. The leader was a big, bearded man called Messiter. I've never seen Messiter in Calico, but the Mexican looked familiar. I think I've seen him in town now and again, probably getting supplies.

'We didn't tell you earlier about seeing Vickery,' the doctor went on, 'because I was scared of what they might do to my wife. But we've talked about it since then, and even though we're still scared, we figured we should do everything we can to help you hand those outlaws out there over to the law.'

'You've already given us all the information we need to know,' said Jim. 'I'm going to send a message to the US marshal at Fort Smith asking him to send deputies to arrest Vickery and the others. I'll ask them to contact you here in Calico. But Fort Smith is a long way off and I've heard that deputies are spread pretty thin in Indian Territory, so we can't be sure how long it's going to be before they turn up.

'I don't want to take the risk of Vickery leaving while we wait for the law to turn up here,' Jim went on, 'so Morgan and me'll have to go after him ourselves, and hand him over to the deputies when they get here. We'll take a room in the hotel and try and work out a plan. We'll let you know what we're going to do, and if you get any more threats, let us know right away. And thanks for telling us what you did.'

Before they left, Jim wrote down the message to the US marshal at Fort Smith, and Sawyer said he would arrange for it to go on the next east-bound stagecoach.

They left Sawyer's house, booked in at the hotel and took a meal, after which they went up to their room.

'I've been thinking,' said Morgan. 'Vickery's only seen me once, for a split second, in a darkened room at the Diamond R. He'd never recognize me from that meeting. What if we work out some way for me to ride in on him and join up with him and Parker? With me on the inside, we'd have a better chance of doing what we want to do.'

'That would be mighty dangerous for you, Morgan, alone in the middle of a bunch of seven outlaws,' said Jim. 'You sure you want to try it?'

'I'm sure,' replied Morgan.

They spent the next two hours devising a plan for the operation, the implementation of which depended partly on the result of some enquiries they had to make the following day. Then they both turned in.

The following morning, after breakfast, they went to see the doctor and his wife and gave them the outline of their plan. Then Jim asked Sawyer if there was somebody in town with a wide knowledge of the surrounding area.

'That would be Walter Hadley,' said Sawyer. 'He's a patient of mine, not long recovered from a bad attack of pneumonia. He's lived in these parts longer than anybody else around here. I think he did a lot of prospecting around here in his younger days, but he never found anything worthwhile. He's a friend of mine, as well as a patient, I'll take you along to see him, if you want.'

'Thanks,' said Jim, and he and Morgan followed the doctor out of the house and along the street to a small shack on the edge of town.

'Just a minute,' said Sawyer, then knocked and went inside. He came out a few minutes later.

'I'll leave you now,' he said. 'You can go in and see Walter. I hope he'll be able to tell you what you want to know.'

Walter Hadley was a short slim man in his sixties. He greeted them with a toothless grin and waved them over to two chairs.

'The doc's a good friend of mine,' he said. 'How can I help?'

'I'm asking you to imagine,' said Jim, 'that you're an outlaw leader being chased by the law. You and seven men have come over the border from Kansas, and you're looking for a cave with a narrow entrance where you can hide out for a spell. Can you think of any place between here and the border where you'd find what you wanted?'

Hadley cast his mind back over the years.

'A big cave with a small entrance, you said. Can't think of one offhand.' He scratched his head and half-closed his eyes. His brow furrowed in concentration. Then he banged his fist on the arm of his chair.

'I've just remembered,' he said. 'Nigh on twenty years ago I came on a cave like that, just by accident, and spent a few nights in it. The entrance was easily big enough for a man to walk through, and it was well hidden by brush. Inside, I recollect, there was a good area of floor, and the ceiling was nine or ten feet high.'

'Where is this cave?' asked Jim.

'In the wall of a ravine,' replied Hadley, 'roughly north-east of here, maybe twenty miles away, not far south of the Kansas border. I can tell you exactly where to find it. I can still remember the landmarks around there.'

'That sounds just like the sort of place we're interested in,' said Jim. 'We're going to take a ride out there right now to have a look at it. We'd be obliged if you didn't mention our talk to anybody.'

'Don't worry,' said Hadley. 'Doc Sawyer already asked me to keep quiet about it.'

After getting directions from Hadley, Jim and Morgan headed for the ravine, and arrived there in the afternoon. Riding inside it, they could see no sign of a cave entrance, but following Hadley's directions they rode up to a dense mass of brush growing against the wall of the ravine.

They dismounted, forced their way into the brush, and after a brief search, found the cave entrance. They pushed through the brush which was growing in front of it, and paused for a moment while Jim lit an oil lamp he had brought with him.

In front of them was a narrow passage about six and a half feet high, leading into the wall of the ravine. They followed this for eighteen feet, when it curved a little bit to the left, and after another six feet, opened out into a roughly circular area about eight yards in diameter, with a nine-foot-high ceiling. There were no signs of recent habitation, but Jim felt sure that it had been occupied at some time in the long-distant past.

They examined the area closely, then walked back to the cave entrance, which Jim examined closely while Morgan pulled the brush aside.

'Just big enough to get a horse through,' commented Jim. 'It's even better than I hoped. You remember we were thinking of holding a couple of guns on the outlaws from the outside. Well, I've just had a better idea. Looking at this entrance, you can see it would be easy to close it with a metal grid. That way, we wouldn't have to be watching it all the time.'

While Morgan held the brush away from the entrance, Jim took some detailed measurements of the opening. Then they rode back to Calico.

Early next morning, they went to see Sawyer.

They told him that they had found a place which fitted ideally into their plans, but they needed a metal grid to be made for closing the cave entrance. Jim asked the doctor if there was anyone in town who would make this for them.

'The blacksmith, Dwight Warner, would do it for you,' said Sawyer. 'He and his wife are patients of mine, and good friends as well. Would you like me to ask him to come over?'

'I'd be obliged,' said Jim. 'If our plan's going to work, we've got to get that grid made, and out to the ravine, as quick as we can.'

Ten minutes later, the doctor came back with Warner, and introduced him to Jim and Morgan. The blacksmith was a stocky, bearded man, with powerful arms.

'Dwight knows about the urgency of the work,' said Sawyer, 'and he knows that you're aiming to catch some outlaws and hand them over to the law. He's willing to help you as much as he can, and to keep quiet about it.'

Jim thanked the blacksmith and told him that he wanted a metal grid which could be used to close the entrance to a cave about twenty miles north-east of Calico in which a number of armed men were to be held prisoner.

He gave Warner the exact measurements he had taken, and explained that the grid must be strong enough to withstand gunfire at close quarters; and must be designed so that the sliding bolts he was asking for on one side of the door should not be capable of being withdrawn by an arm reaching through the grid from inside the cave.

Warner studied the measurements before he replied.

'I've got all the materials to do the job,' he said. 'I'll start on it first thing in the morning. Could probably finish it by dark. It's going to weigh pretty heavy. I reckon the best way to get it out there will be on a travois. I'll build a simple one for the job. Then we could take it out of town after dark, when nobody's around.'

'You figure on coming along with us?' asked Jim.

'I do,' replied Warner. 'Maybe that grid'll have to be trimmed a bit to make it fit proper, and eight holes'll need to be chiselled in the rock at the sides of that cave entrance. You'll need some help with those. We could leave here around midnight and start on the work at the cave at daybreak.'

'We sure do appreciate all the help you're giving us,' said Jim. 'Can we help you with the work on the grid?'

'Come to the shop at daylight,' said the blacksmith. 'You can work on the travois while I work on the grid.'

The work was finished by early evening on the following day, and just before midnight, Jim and Morgan, accompanied by Warner, rode, unnoticed, out of town. The blacksmith, mounted on his own horse, was leading another horse drawing the travois, with the metal grid lashed to it.

They arrived while it was still dark, and waited for daybreak before starting work. They found that very little additional work was necessary on the grid, and when this had been carried out they set about using the hammers and chisels that Warner had brought with him to make the necessary holes in the two rock walls of the passage leading into the cave.

The holes in one wall accommodated the ends of four of the horizontal bars of the grid; those in the other wall accommodated the ends of the four sliding bolts when they were pushed home.

After several hours of hard work, interrupted by a break at noon, Warner pronounced himself satisfied.

'When those bolts are pushed home,' he said, 'nobody could get out of there without the proper tools.'

'They couldn't shoot their way out?' asked Morgan.

'Not a chance,' replied Warner. 'Not the way I've built it.'

They hid the grid in the brush three yards to one side of the entrance, and arranged the brush at the entrance so that it concealed the holes in the walls. Then they returned to Calico, arriving after dark.

Jim thanked Warner, then he and Morgan went to the hotel for a meal, after which they went up to their room to discuss plans for the following day.

'Like I mentioned when we were working on the plan before,' said Jim, 'the best way for you to get taken on by Vickery is to pretend that you know one of his men. I think that man should be Rothery, one of the men you shot dead in the Diamond R ranch house. The reason being that when they had me buried in that ravine with my head sticking out of the ground, Rothery and Gardner were sitting close by me for a spell and Rothery was yarning to Gardner about his past. I could hear everything they were saying.'

'You'd better fill me in then,' said Morgan. 'I already know what he looked like.'

'Right,' said Jim. 'His first name was Ken. His parents live on a farm near Liberty, Missouri. Three months ago, he left the Vickery gang for three weeks to visit them. Before he joined up with the Vickery gang he worked on his own, mostly on stagecoach robberies, but he wasn't doing too well and he figured he'd be better off in a bigger outfit. So he managed to get in touch with Vickery through a mutual friend called Milt Lester.

'And that's about it,' Jim concluded. 'I reckon you'd better ride out to Vickery's place tomorrow. I'll wait here till I hear from you how things are going.'

'I'll make some excuse to ride into Calico,' said Morgan. 'I'll let you know then.'

ELEVEN

Morgan rode out of Calico early the next morning, and following Sawyer's directions he had no difficulty in locating the outlaws' hideout. As he rode up to the mouth of the ravine, a look-out armed with a rifle walked out from behind a nearby boulder and challenged him.

'That's far enough, stranger,' he said. 'Who are you, and what d'you want?'

'The name's Rob Garner,' said Morgan, 'and I'm looking for an old friend of mine called Ken Rothery. I figured I might find him here.'

'He ain't here,' said the look-out, 'but there is somebody here who'll want a word with you. I'll take your gun.'

Morgan hesitated for a moment, then handed the gun over.

'Walk over to the nearest cabin,' said the look-out. 'I'll be right behind you.'

When they reached the cabin, the look-out opened the door, pushed Morgan inside, and followed him in. There were two men inside, sitting on armchairs. One of them Morgan recognized, from Jim's description, as Vickery. His shoulder was bandaged. The other one he recognized, from Sawyer's description, as Messiter. The two gang-leaders eyed Morgan with suspicion.

The look-out spoke to Vickery. 'This man just rode in bold as brass,' he said. 'Says his name's Rob Garner. Asked if he could see Ken Rothery.'

Vickery scowled. 'Just who are you?' he asked. 'And what's your business with Rothery?'

'I'm a friend of Ken's,' Morgan replied. 'We grew up together. Our parents were farming close together near Liberty, Missouri. I guess you must be Mr Vickery. Ken told me about you the last time I saw him.'

'When was that?' asked Vickery.

'About three months ago,' Morgan replied, 'when he was visiting his folks near Liberty.'

'And just what brought you here?' asked Vickery.

'Well,' said Morgan, 'I guess you know that before Ken joined up with you, he used to work on his own – robbing stagecoaches mostly. I did the same thing myself. We joined up for a couple of jobs that were too big for one man to handle. Then I lost touch with him until I met him again in Missouri three months ago.

'He told me,' Morgan went on, 'that he'd joined up with you and was making a sight more money than he ever did on his own. He said that if ever I

felt like doing the same thing I should come here
on the chance that the gang might be resting up,
and he'd put in a good word for me.'

'He told you exactly where to find us?' asked
Vickery.

'Yes, he did,' Morgan replied. 'Mind you, he said
to be darned sure I didn't mention this hideout to
anybody else. Made me swear to it.'

'So you reckon you'd like to work with us?'
asked Vickery.

'I sure would,' Morgan replied. 'What happened
was that I was chased across the Kansas border
by a posse a week ago and I holed up for a few
days in a cave that I knew of, about five miles
south of the border. While I was there I got to
thinking that Ken had done the sensible thing, so
I hightailed it down here to see him. Is he
around?'

'He's dead,' said Vickery. 'Got killed in a shoot-
out in the Texas Panhandle a few weeks ago.'

Morgan looked severely taken aback by the
news. 'I'm sorry to hear that,' he said. 'Ken and
me, we go back a long ways. Like I said, I was
hoping he'd put in a good word for me. I know you
can't take on just anybody who comes along.
Thanks for your time. If I can have my gun back,
I'll be on my way.'

He turned towards the look-out, holding his
hand out for his revolver.

'Just a minute,' said Vickery. 'I'm mighty short-
handed just now, and I need more men. I'm

expecting two to join me soon, but I could do with one more. As soon as this shoulder's healed up, we're riding to the Texas Panhandle to settle accounts with the people who killed some of my men, including Ken and my nephew. Maybe you'd like to join us?'

'I sure would,' said Morgan, and took back his gun from the look-out.

Vickery chatted with Morgan for a while, the latter drawing on his imagination to provide information on a few minor robberies he had perpetrated in the past. Then Messiter took him over to one of the cabins, which was occupied by Vickery's man, Parker, the half-breed. On the way he spotted three men, presumably members of Messiter's gang, standing outside one of the cabins. One of them was a Mexican.

Inside Parker's cabin was a spare bunk which Messiter told Morgan to use, after introducing him to Parker as a new member of Vickery's gang. Chatting with Parker, Morgan was relieved to find that he knew little of Rothery's life prior to his joining the gang.

The day passed slowly for Morgan and he was glad when the time came to turn in. As he lay on his bunk he decided that he would ride into Calico the following day to see Jim and trigger the next stage of the plan.

Just around daylight, he was disturbed by Parker, who left his bunk, dressed, and walked out of the shack. Morgan dozed for a while, then got up himself and went to the cookshack for breakfast. After the meal he walked over to the cabin occupied by the two gang-leaders and knocked on the door. A shout from the other side told him to enter.

Vickery and Messiter were seated inside. Morgan spoke to Vickery.

'I'd like to ride into Calico to buy me some new boots,' he said. 'The ones I've got on have never fitted me proper. They're just about crippling me. You reckon they'll have some in the store there?'

'Sure,' said Vickery, 'but it's a pity you didn't mention this earlier. Parker rode into Calico a couple of hours ago to get some things from the store. He needn't have gone if we'd known you were figuring to go yourself. If Parker's still in town when you get there tell him to get back as quick as he can. And the same goes for you too. I don't like my men hanging around there any longer than they have to.'

Though considerably alarmed by the news that Parker had ridden into Calico, which raised the possibility that he might see and recognize Jim, Morgan kept his face expressionless as he nodded and left the cabin. He decided that he must get to Calico as quickly as possible.

When Parker reached Calico, he went into the store and stood at the counter, waiting until a customer already in there had been served. Turning his head, he took a casual look across the street. A man who had just walked out of the door of the hotel opposite, stood on the boardwalk, looking up and down the street.

Immediately, Parker recognized the man as Jim Cochrane. He stiffened, and watched as Jim turned and went back into the hotel. He waited a few minutes, then left the store without being served, and walked quickly over to the hotel entrance, rubbing his brow with his hand so as to partially screen his face.

Walking into the hotel, he found the lobby empty. He peered through a glass door into the dining-room and located Jim, seated at a table at the far side of the room, with his back to the door.

Parker stepped away from the door and looked around the lobby. It was still empty. He walked to the desk, spun the register round, and looked inside it. He saw the name 'Jim Cochrane', and against it 'Room 5'. He spun the register back, then ran up the stairs and along the corridor at the top until he reached Room 5. He turned the door knob, pushed the door open, and went inside.

When Jim had finished his meal he left the dining-room and started climbing the stairs to his room. Half-way up, he remembered that he needed to buy a new bandanna to replace the one he was wearing, which had been accidentally damaged.

He turned, descended the stairs, and walked across to the store on the opposite side of the street. Five minutes later he left, wearing the new

bandanna, and walked across towards the hotel.
As he glanced along the street he fancied that he
saw, out of the corner of his eye, a movement on
the other side of the window of his hotel room.

Suppressing an impulse to look directly up at
the window, he continued across the street and
went into the hotel. He was fairly certain that
somebody was in his room, and wondered who it
could be. It might be Morgan, or it might be somebody waiting to ambush him.

Darby, the hotel owner, was at the desk in the
lobby as Jim passed through, heading for his
room. Half-way up the stairs he checked his
Peacemaker and held it in his hand, ready to fire.
He climbed the rest of the stairs and walked along
the corridor at the top. It was not carpeted and he
knew that the sound of footsteps along the corridor was clearly audible in the rooms.

He stopped just before he was outside the door
of his own room, and stretched out his left hand to
grasp the door knob. As he started to turn it, there
came from inside the room the sound of a rapid
succession of four revolver shots, and four bullets
slammed, at chest height, through the flimsy
panelling of the door, with barely reduced velocity,
and buried themselves in the wall of the corridor
opposite.

Jim let out what he hoped was a realistic shout
of pain, followed by a loud groan and a heavy
thump as he banged his foot hard on the floor.
Then, gun in hand, he lay motionless on his right

side along the corridor, with only his legs stretch-
ing across the doorway. His gun, held in his right
hand, was concealed under his body.

Parker pulled the door open, saw Jim's legs,
peered around the door-jamb at the motionless
body on the floor, then quickly stepped out,
revolver in hand, and bent over Jim, intending to
shoot him through the head. Miraculously, Jim's
Peacemaker suddenly appeared in sight and he
shot Parker in the chest, over the heart. The
outlaw's gun fell from his hand and he collapsed
on the floor of the corridor.

Jim checked that the outlaw was dead, then
turned to face Darby, the hotel owner as, moving
with caution, he appeared at the top of the stairs.
He beckoned Darby along the corridor, and
showed him the bullet-holes in the door and the
wall.

'Those bullets were meant for me,' he said. 'This
man was hiding in my room. Lucky I suspected
there was somebody in there. He's an outlaw
called Parker. I've been following the trail of him
and his boss.'

Darby examined the door and the points where
the bullets were embedded in the wall opposite.

'Looks like you were plumb lucky,' he observed.
'You a lawman?'

'I was once, but not now,' replied Jim. 'This is
personal. Is there somebody in town who can take
care of the body?'

'Dwight Warner's your man,' said Darby. 'I'll

send somebody to go and ask him to come over.'

'Thanks,' said Jim. 'I'll notify the marshal in Fort Smith that Parker is dead.'

They both went downstairs, and Jim told Darby that he was going to the doctor's house. He was half-way there when he saw Morgan riding fast into town. He waited while his friend rode up to him, and they stood on the boardwalk while he told Morgan about his recent encounter with Parker.

'Lucky you spotted him in your room,' said Morgan, then went on to tell his friend that his story had been accepted by Vickery, who had invited him to join his gang.

'That's good,' said Jim. 'I reckon we should start things moving right away.'

They had a lengthy discussion about the next stage of their plan, then Morgan headed for the outlaws' hideout, while Jim walked along to Sawyer's house. The doctor and his wife were both at home.

They invited him inside, and he told them about Parker's death. He said that the plan was progressing well, and that he and Morgan would both be out of town for a while. It was unlikely, he told them, that any US deputy marshals would turn up for a while in response to Jim's message, but if they did, he asked Sawyer to tell them to wait in town till he or Morgan returned.

Morgan rode at a normal pace until he was two

miles from the outlaws' hideout. Then he urged his mount into a gallop, and maintained a fast pace until he rode into the ravine and up to Vickery's cabin. He brought his labouring mount to a sliding stop, jumped down and hammered on the cabin door, then opened it and ran inside. Those gang members who had observed his hasty arrival ran up to the cabin.

Vickery and Messiter stared at Morgan as he burst in on them. Both rose to their feet.

'What's up?' asked Vickery.

'We ain't got much time,' said Morgan. 'We've got to get out of here.' He went on to tell them, speaking as fast as he could, that he had met Parker in the store in Calico, and had left him inside, the only customer. Then, standing by his horse, and looking over its back, he had seen a group of ten US deputy marshals riding into town.

Ducking down, he had crawled, unobserved, into a narrow space under the boarded sidewalk, where he lay, motionless. He could see the horses' and men's legs as the deputies stopped outside the store and dismounted.

Then he had heard the door of the store opening above him and the sound of Parker stepping out on to the boardwalk, then stopping suddenly as he saw the group of lawmen in front of him.

Morgan went on to tell Vickery and Messiter that he had heard one of the deputies yelling, 'I know that man. He's an outlaw called Rufus

Parker. He's one of the Vickery gang.' The deputy in charge of the group had called on Parker to surrender, but he tried to make a run for it, and was cut down before he reached his horse. Morgan had seen his body lying on the ground.

'What happened then?' asked Vickery.

'The body was carried away,' replied Morgan, 'and the deputies stood by the store, talking for a while. I was close enough to hear what they were saying. Seems like they'd been sent to make a search of the area for outlaws and outlaw hide-outs, and after they'd checked up on everybody in town, which wouldn't take long, they were going to have a meal in the hotel, and after that they were going to start a search of the area around Calico.

'I waited where I was,' Morgan went on, ''till I saw them all go into the hotel dining-room. Then I crawled out from under the boardwalk when nobody was looking, and hightailed it out here just as fast as I could.'

Vickery's face was dark with anger.

'After what they did to Rufus,' he said, 'I'd like the chance of shooting a few of them down. But there's too many for us to take on. How long d'you think it'll be before they turn up here?'

'It's hard to say,' said Morgan. 'I don't know how they were going to carry out the search. But the way they were talking, they'll be passing through here sometime soon. Maybe they'll be here later today, maybe tomorrow. But I reckon we should play safe by leaving just as soon as we can.'

Abruptly, Messiter left the cabin, and told one of the men outside to alert the look-out, then ride to a piece of high ground nearby and keep a close watch for approaching riders, particularly from the north-west. Then he returned to the cabin.

'I've put another man on watch,' he told Vickery.

Vickery turned to Morgan. 'I reckon you're right about leaving soon,' he said, and Messiter nodded agreement. 'The question is,' Vickery went on, 'just where do we go from here? This shoulder of mine ain't healed properly yet and I don't think a lot of riding would do it any good.'

'It's clear,' said Messiter, 'that if we want to keep away from those deputies, we'd better ride north and find a place somewhere near the Kansas border where we can hide out for a spell.'

Morgan was just about to suggest to them that the cave he had told them about on his arrival might do, when Vickery turned to him.

'Just a minute,' he said. 'Didn't you say that on your way down here you'd holed up in a cave near the border?'

'That's right,' said Morgan.

'Is it big enough to take all of us?' asked Vickery.

'Sure,' said Morgan, 'and the horses as well if we wanted to hide them for a spell. And there's good grazing nearby. But the best thing about it is that when the brush is pulled back across the entrance, nobody passing by can tell there's a cave there at all.'

'That sounds just the place for us,' said Vickery.

'I'm not so sure,' said Messiter. 'Maybe with all those US deputy marshals around, we should ride right out of Indian Territory.'

'Don't forget,' said Vickery, 'that we're wanted just as badly in Kansas, and it ain't so easy to find a place to hide there. Let's head for the cave, and if I feel like riding any further when we get there, we'll ride on to Kansas. If this shoulder's acting up, we'll stay in the cave.'

Messiter agreed to this, and he and Vickery went outside to explain the situation to the men and to tell them to be ready to leave in an hour's time. Messiter told one of his men, Stevens, to make sure they took along some oil lamps and coal-oil, in case they decided to stay in the cave.

TWELVE

They left an hour later, carrying provisions for
several days with them, and heading for the cave.
As they neared it, late in the evening, Morgan
took the lead, and finally located the ravine in the
dark. He paused at the entrance to the ravine and
spoke to Vickery.

'The cave's up there,' he said, 'about a hundred
yards on the right, in the wall of the ravine. Do we
go up there, or carry on over the border?'

Vickery groaned. 'This shoulder hurts like hell,'
he said. 'I ain't riding no more today. We'll stay
here.'

Morgan led the way up the ravine and stopped
near the cave.

'We're there,' he said. as he dismounted. The
others followed suit.

'We'd better light some lamps,' said Morgan.

Stevens produced three lamps and lit them. He
handed Vickery and Messiter one each, and gave
the other to Morgan, who pushed his way through

the brush to the concealed entrance and pulled the greenery aside to reveal it.

He called down to the others to come up, and Vickery and Messiter, each carrying a lamp, led the way. The others followed close behind, with Stevens at the end of the line.

'The cave's at the end of the passage,' said Morgan, as Vickery passed him.

Curious to see the interior of the cave, the men followed the two gang-leaders along the passage. Stevens had just stepped inside it, when he turned.

'I'd better tie my horse up tight,' he said. 'It's been a bit skittish lately. I don't want it running off.'

He walked past Morgan, who turned quickly and rapped the outlaw on the back of his head with the barrel of his Peacemaker, then eased him to the ground. Morgan placed the oil lamp on the ground at the side of the entrance and quickly dragged the unconscious Stevens a few feet into the passage. Then he ran out and stood just outside the entrance.

'Now, Jim,' he called softly.

Three yards to the right of the entrance there was a rustling sound in the brush as Jim emerged, dragging behind him the heavy metal grid which the blacksmith in Calico had fashioned.

Morgan ran up to help him and together they dragged the grid up to the cave entrance and stood it upright. Then, working as quickly as they could, they slid the projecting rods on one side of the grid into the holes in the wall which had been prepared for them.

Positioning the grid, they then slid the bolts into the holes in the opposite wall. As Morgan slid the last bolt home, he saw someone holding a lamp walking along the passage towards them. They both moved sideways away from the entrance, in order to avoid any gunfire, and stood up against the ravine wall.

Moments later, when the unconscious Stevens and the grid were discovered, there came a volley of curses from the passage, followed by a babel of voices and the sound of the grid being violently shaken. Eventually the noise died down, and the two men outside heard somebody calling out. They recognized the voice as Vickery's.

'You there, Garner?' he asked.

Jim replied. 'This is Cochrane,' he said. 'My friend Morgan Jenkins, alias Rob Garner, is here with me. You and the others have reached the end of the road, Vickery. I'm expecting a posse of US deputy marshals here soon, to take you all away for trial.'

'Damn you, Cochrane!' said Vickery. 'I should've shot you through the head before I left you with Bellamy in the Panhandle. Don't forget we're all armed. Anybody comes in sight of this door, and we'll shoot them dead.'

'I don't think that'll happen,' said Jim. 'A couple

of riflemen out here should be able to keep you away from the door. I don't figure there's any need for a gun battle. You've got no feed and water in there. All those deputies need to do is hang around here till you all give yourselves up.'

Vickery made no reply, but Jim and Morgan heard the sound of angry voices coming from the cave entrance. They moved a few yards further down the ravine, out of earshot of the prisoners.

'Come daylight, I'm going to ride to Calico,' said Jim, 'to let Sawyer know that we've got the outlaws fastened in the cave. I guess it'll be a relief for them. I'll tell them that when the deputy US marshals turn up, they should ask them to ride out here to pick up the prisoners, warning them to wait for one of us before they ride up the ravine. I should be back in the afternoon.'

'Right,' said Morgan. 'I'll have to remember to keep out of sight of that cave entrance. There's a lot of guns in there.'

Jim and Morgan slept little for the rest of the night, listening to the bursts of argument and profanity coming from the cave entrance.

Jim left at dawn. When he reached Calico he gave the Sawyers the good news that the threat from the outlaws had been removed. He told Sawyer what he wanted him to do when the lawmen appeared. Then he rode back to join Morgan.

When he arrived back at the ravine, Morgan told him that the outlaws had been firing at the rods in the grid which extended into the holes in the wall. But eventually they had obviously realized that all they were doing was wasting ammunition.

Two days later, earlier than Jim had expected, four deputy US marshals turned up, led by Deputy Marshal Hendry. Jim led them into the ravine and explained the situation to them.

'This is quite a catch,' said Hendry. 'These are all outlaws we've been after for a long time. Vickery and Messiter'll hang, for certain, together with some of the others. There's a jail wagon following on behind us. Should be here maybe tomorrow. Then we can take them in for trial. By the time it gets here, maybe they'll have given themselves up.'

'I've been thinking about that,' said Jim. 'I guess you don't want to hang around here too long.'

He picked up a small tuft of grass and threw it into the air. A stiff breeze carried it directly towards the wall of the ravine in which the cave entrance was located.

'Why not speed things up a bit? Why don't we smoke them out?' he asked.

'That's a good idea,' said Hendry.

Standing to one side of the cave entrance, out of danger of gunfire from within, they threw a big pile of loose, dry brush on to the ground close to the grid, then cast a burning piece of brush on top to ignite it. When it was burning well, they threw a quantity of green foliage on top of it.

Smoke, billowing from the pile, was blown through the grid, along the passage, and into the cave, where the outlaws had collected. Outside, the lawmen kept the fire going.

It was some time before enough smoke had entered to fill the cave, but eventually the outlaws, coughing uncontrollably, appeared behind the grid.

'I want every gun thrown out here,' shouted Hendry, and not until six revolvers had been dropped outside through the grid, did he draw back the bolts and allow the outlaws, choking, and gasping for breath, to stagger past the fire and out of the smoke into the open.

The fire was quickly put out, and some time later, when the smoke had cleared from the inside of the cave, the outlaws were returned there and locked in pending the arrival of the jail wagon. Meanwhile, Jim and Morgan returned to Calico.

Subsequently, Vickery and Messiter and two gang members died on the gallows. The other two outlaws received long custodial sentences.

Before they left for the Texas Panhandle the following morning, Jim arranged for a telegraph message to be sent to the Rangers in Linford, telling them that Vickery was in custody, and that they could return to the ranch. It also told them that he and Morgan were on their way back to the Diamond R.

Three days after they left Calico, Jim and his

friend rode up to the Diamond R ranch house. Miriam ran out as they dismounted.

'We've been watching out for you two,' she said. 'Welcome back.'

Don Martin walked over to greet them, and they all walked into the house, where they joined Emily Ranger and Joey, and where Jim and Morgan recounted the full story of the downfall of Vickery and the others.

'Looks like you really outfoxed them,' said Don.

'We owe you both a lot,' said Emily Ranger. 'We sure are glad to be back on the ranch again. And we're really grateful to Don and the two hands for helping us out.'

Later, Jim had the chance of a word alone with Miriam.

'What does your mother think of the idea of having me as a son-in-law?' he asked.

'She reckons I'd be on to a good thing,' smiled Miriam, 'provided I can tame you down a bit and get you settled into a quieter way of life. And as for you helping to run the place, she's all in favour of the idea.'

Jim kissed her. 'In that case,' he said, 'let's go and have a talk with her.'